THE LEGEND OF JACK DONOVAN

BAILEY CLAN WESTERNS
BOOK ONE

TERENCE NEWNES

Copyright © 2024 by Terence Newnes

Layout design and Copyright © 2024 by Next Chapter

Published 2024 by Next Chapter

Cover art by Jaylord Bonnit

This book is a work of fiction. Names, characters, places, and incidents are the product of the author's imagination or are used fictitiously. Any resemblance to actual events, locales, or persons, living or dead, is purely coincidental.

All rights reserved. No part of this book may be reproduced or transmitted in any form or by any means, electronic or mechanical, including photocopying, recording, or by any information storage and retrieval system, without the author's permission.

This book is for my family:
For my wife; you are the force behind my writing.
For my daughter; may you always be strong.
For my son; you have the Bailey spirit, family first.

CHAPTER 1
THE STRANGER

He rode into town from the west. It was evening, and the setting sun was behind him as he rode. A tall, dusty man on a tall, dusty horse, riding easily in the saddle as he walked his horse down the dusty main street, with another horse on a lead rope tied to the pommel of his saddle. In fact, it was the only street of the town, if it could even be called that. It was just a cleared expanse of dried mud, which would turn into a morass when the rains came. It had never been graded and probably never would. The town itself consisted of the usual false-fronted buildings lining the street on both sides. There was a hotel offering food and rooms for rent, a general store, some office buildings, the marshal's office next to the jail, and the usual saloons. Some distance away from the commercial buildings were the residential buildings of the town's inhabitants: log cabins, adobe houses, some shacks, and even a few dugouts in the hillside. The town went by the name of Cedar Creek, and its sign boasted a population of 548, which included the surrounding cattle ranches. The stranger noted all this as he slowly rode down the street. He was a man accustomed to being alert and wary of his surroundings.

The stranger tied the horses to the hitching rail in front of the First Chance Saloon and jerked his rifle from its sheath. Banging his hat against his clothes to remove some of the accumulated trail dust, he mounted the boardwalk to the batwing doors. His keen blue eyes looked tired but still alert as he surveyed the interior of the saloon and the people who were there. There was a long bar taking up one side of the room, and a few tables were scattered around with chairs. Two hard-looking men were at the bar, dressed like cowboys, but the stranger immediately pegged them as gunslingers for hire. He had seen a few in his time. There were other men at the bar, but he figured them to be locals. There were townspeople seated at tables as well, but his attention was drawn to a table where four men were playing cards. Two of them he took to be professional gamblers. The third was a tough-looking man who shaped up to be a miner. The fourth was a young man, barely 20 years old. A good-looking youngster with long blond hair, he appeared to be on the way to being drunk, with a half-empty glass of whiskey at his elbow.

The stranger pushed the batwing doors apart and walked into the saloon. Everyone looked up to see who the newcomer was. They saw a tall, well-built man in his late twenties with broad shoulders and a slim waist, dressed in the usual range clothing with a flat-crowned black hat. He wore a low-slung, tied-down gun on his right thigh, and from the looks of the worn and polished gun butt and holster, both had seen much use. He carried his Henry rifle as though it were an extension of his left arm. His face looked drawn and tired, but the blue eyes were still alert. He had an angular face, hard-looking but with good features; and while he could never be called handsome, there was character in that face that made it attractive. As he entered, the young man looked up and caught his eye. The young man started to get up and began to say something like,

"Ja...," but even though he was startled, he caught the almost imperceptible shake of the stranger's head and subsided in his seat.

The stranger walked up to the bar, and when the barkeep came over, he slapped a coin on the counter and said, "Whiskey, a double, and not that rotgut you usually serve. Pour it from the bottle under the counter." The barkeep stared at him for a moment and was about to protest, but then he looked into the stranger's eyes, and not liking what he saw, he pulled out a bottle from under the counter and poured the stranger a double. The stranger downed the drink in a single swallow and sighed. "That sure does settle the dust," he commented. "The same again." The barkeep poured him another double, and the stranger picked it up and then turned around to face the room, leaning his back against the bar. He still held his rifle in his left hand and the drink in his right as he watched the four men playing cards at the table.

Suddenly, the miner slammed his fist on the table and snarled, "Someone here is cheating for sure!" He glared at the young man and said, "Maybe it's you, kid! You seem to be winning a lot just when I'm losing!" The young man turned slightly pale, but he gave the miner a level look and said, "In this country, it's an insult to call a man a cheat. But I'm giving you the chance to take them words back." The miner stood up and snarled, "Like hell I will! You're a cheat!" Without taking his eyes off the miner, the young man slowly stood up, and his hand dropped to his gun. "Whenever you're ready," he said. The miner looked confused, as the youngster now appeared to be stone-cold sober, and he threw a glance at the two hard-looking men at the bar. Then he challenged the young man, saying, "I'm no gunfighter, but I'll tear you apart with my bare hands if you have the guts." The young man smiled wryly and told him, "I'm no gunfighter myself. But seeing as how it was you who insulted me, I figure I get the right to choice of weapon, so draw when you're ready." He paused and then added harshly, "Either draw or eat your words right here, right now!" The miner again threw a glance at the two men at the bar, and one of them nodded his head slightly. He turned back to the young man and said, "Okay then, kid, this is where you get yours!" In the absolute silence of the room, as everyone waited for the explosive action to start, the click of the rifle hammer seemed extraordinarily loud. "You two gentlemen just turn around and face the bar," the stranger said without raising his voice.

With everyone's attention focused on the unfolding scene at the table, the stranger had unobtrusively placed his glass on the counter and had turned his body slightly so that he now had the two hard-looking men on his left under his rifle, while his right hand could draw his six-gun and point it towards the table or towards the two men at the bar. Having caught the nod that one of the men gave the miner, the stranger realized that this was a setup for a kill, and the young man was the target. Hearing the click of the hammer and the stranger's words, the two men half turned towards him with their hands dropping to their gun butts, only to find the barrel of the rifle pointing unwaveringly straight at them. "I wouldn't," was all the stranger said, but it froze their hands all the same. One of them blustered, "What the hell, mister, we didn't do nothing, so why the hell are you pointing a gun at us?"

The stranger sighed and said, "Either face the bar, gentlemen, or I'll put a bullet through the two of you. This here is a Henry, and believe me, it can do the job with one bullet. Now!" Cursing, the two men turned and faced the bar. "Hands on the bar, gentlemen!" the stranger added. "I wouldn't want to lead you into temptation!" Cursing again, the two men complied and placed their hands on the bar. Taking a step away from the bar, the stranger told the barkeep, "Do me a favor and move over and face them." The barkeep shrugged and moved until he was in front of the men. The stranger then told the two gamblers, "Gentlemen, do you have a stake in this? If you do, draw your cards and we'll see how they lay; if not, then I would be mighty pleased if you would place your hands on the table." The two gamblers hastily placed their hands prominently on the table. "Mister, we got nothing to do with whatever this is," one of them said. The stranger nodded agreeably, and looking at the miner, he said, "Well now, you're free to draw, so go ahead and show the kid what you got." The miner looked stunned at the turn of events, and he blustered, "I'm no gunslinger, but I'll tear him apart with my bare hands if he has the guts to face me!"

One of the men at the bar was slowly, and as he figured, unobtrusively sliding his right hand off the bar to drop it and grab his gun. The stranger casually raised his rifle slightly, and a shot rang out. The man screamed and clutched his right hand with his left. He turned around, and everyone could see that the bullet had gone through the center of his palm. The other man half-turned but turned back immediately when he saw the rifle barrel centered on him. "Both of you drop your gun belts right now," the stranger ordered. The injured man moaned, "Hell, you shot my hand; how am I supposed to do that?" The stranger gave an indifferent shrug and said, "Use your left hand, unless you want a bullet through that as well!" Cursing, both the men unbuckled their gun belts and let them drop to the ground. "How about you?" the stranger asked the barkeep. "You want to draw some chips in this game?"

"I ain't a fool, mister. I ain't going to argue with a rifle," the barkeep said, and placed both his hands on the counter. "Wise choice," the stranger said. Then he told the miner, "Either draw or get down on your knees and tell the kid that you're a liar." The miner turned red in the face and snarled, "You'll have to kill me first!" To be branded a liar was the worst insult in the West at the time, where a man's word was his bond, and most deals were done with just a handshake. Nobody would have anything to do with a known liar. "Have it your way then," the stranger said in an indifferent tone of voice, as though he was discussing the weather, and a gun suddenly appeared in his right hand. The gamblers would later swear that they never saw him draw, but that one moment the gun was in his holster and the next it was in his hand. The miner's face turned pale, and he fell to his knees. "Please, mister, I was just funnin'. I didn't mean anything. They paid me to do it," he said, pointing to the two men at the bar. "Doesn't let you off the hook," the stranger replied coldly. "You were willing to be a part of a cowardly murder, so tell the kid that you're a liar, or I'll shoot you right now!" He thumbed back the hammer of the revolver, and the click seemed to galvanize the miner. He screamed, "I'm a liar! I'm a liar!"

"Take his gun, Kid," the stranger told the young man. "And pick up the guns of these two yahoos as well." The injured man was sitting on the ground and tying his bandana around his palm, but the other man snarled, "Big man when you got the drop! I'll find you one of these days, and we'll see how you stack up to a fair shooting."

The young man had taken the miner's gun and was coming to pick up the other two guns when the stranger stopped him. "Stay there and keep everyone covered, Kid," he said. Placing his rifle on the counter and dropping his revolver in his holster, he said, "Judging by what you bushwhackers seemed to have planned here today, I doubt if you know the meaning of the word 'fair.' But okay, tough guy, pick up your gun and let's see what you got." The man's eyes turned wary as he saw that the stranger was still simply standing almost negligently without going into the gunfighter's crouch. "The name's Keegan, you might have heard of me," he said harshly. The stranger shrugged and told him, "Hello and goodbye, Mr. Keegan. They can put that on your tombstone. Now either put up or shut up." Keegan bent and picked up his gun belt and slung it around his hips. Buckling the belt, he adjusted it and then tied down his holster. What happened next became the talk of the town for a long, long time. Pretending to adjust his gun as he was tying down his holster, he suddenly drew with flashing speed. The gamblers and the barkeep would later swear that the stranger just seemed to stand there negligently until Keegan's gun was almost lined up, and then there was a shot and Keegan screamed as the gun fell from his hand. He gripped his wrist and stared at his hand, which was missing the thumb! He screamed again because he knew that his days as a gunslinger were over. The stranger picked up his rifle and backed towards the door. "Let's go, Kid," was all he said.

They rode hard for about two miles, and then the stranger called a halt when they were near the top of a rise. This was hill country, with bare hillsides in some places and thickly covered hillsides in others. It was a rolling land with beautiful grass, ideally suited for cattle ranching. The main water source in the area was Cedar Creek, but there were plenty of other smaller creeks and ponds. They tethered the horses under some junipers near a small spring, and the stranger built a fire, placed a black, beat-up kettle on top of it, and proceeded to heat water for coffee. They hunkered down, and the young man said, "How did you recognize me, Jack? It's been nigh on ten years since you left us, and I was just about ten years old at the time." Jack Donovan, for that was the stranger's name, smiled and said, "Well, Bruce, you look like a younger version of your father, and you have your mother's golden hair. How could I not recognize you? How is your mother, Maria, by the way?" Bruce McCullough sighed and said, "She died during an Indian attack. That was four years ago. We were shorthanded because most of the hands had left to join up to fight the war. There was only Dad, who had just come back wounded from the war, Mum, Beth and myself, and our old cook Thomas, and three of our men who were too old to sign up for the war. Thanks to you, Beth and I could shoot real well, and we gave a good account of ourselves, but when it was over we found that Mum had taken an arrow to the chest, which Dad said had pierced the lung. She died soon after."

CHAPTER 2
JACK DONOVAN

JACK DONOVAN HAD COME OVER THE OREGON TRAIL as a baby with his parents in a covered wagon. The wagon train had been attacked by a roving band of Ute Indians, and both his parents had been killed. Jack was just two years old at the time, and he was taken in by the wagon train scout, a half-white and half-Sioux taciturn man called Ned Falcon, who raised the youngster as his own son. When Jack was old enough to understand, Ned told him of the Indian attack on the wagon train that killed his parents. "You were too young to remember," he told Jack, "but you were sitting right there next to the bodies and holding your mother's hand." Jack asked him, "Why didn't they kill me as well?" Ned shrugged and said, "You can never figure what an Indian might or might not do. The way I read the tracks was this: your parents fought bravely side by side and died bravely. Your father was fatally wounded, but he still managed to knife a young buck who leapt the barricade and attacked him." He pondered for a while and then continued, "I guess that's why your parents weren't scalped, because Indians respect courage. They must have seen you sitting there, but you weren't crying or carrying on; you were just sitting there, which is how you were when I found you. I guess that's why they didn't kill you. They must have figured you to be as brave as your father."

Over the following years, as Jack grew up, Ned Falcon taught him the skills of surviving in the wilderness; tracking, hunting, and using a pistol, rifle, and knife. By the time Jack was twelve years old, he was an expert tracker and hunter, a sharpshooter with a rifle, and as skillful as his adoptive father with a knife. But it was his skill with a pistol that grew much beyond what his adoptive father could teach him. The skill and speed of drawing the pistol and shooting was a natural-born talent for the youngster, and the hours of practice he put in made him a master in the art of the fast draw. He was also deadly accurate in his shooting.

For months at a time they would live off the land, and Jack would virtually be alone. Ned would be along but would hang back and watch everything that the youngster did. At the end of the day, he would point out the things that Jack did wrong and would patiently explain to the youngster how it could have been done better. Making an eight-year-old boy fend for himself in the wilderness may appear harsh to some, but it was a harsh and tough land that they lived in, and you either learned early to survive or you died young. As Ned told Jack, "If anything happens to me, I just want to make sure that you can make out on your own. This is a wild land and a wide-open land, and mostly folks out here are good people. But everyone has their own troubles to attend to, and a body had just better depend on himself and no one else."

Jack was thirteen and big and strong for his age when he and his adoptive father rode into the town of Mesquite in Kansas. The old scout had a weakness for gambling and sat in on a game in the Buckhorn Saloon. Jack sat quietly in a corner and waited patiently for the scout to either break even or go broke. It didn't matter when he went broke because the old scout knew his weakness and always gave Jack a travelling stake to hold before he sat in on any game. Jack had a pistol shoved in his waistband on the right, and he held his rifle in his hands. A knife in a sheath hung down behind his neck between his shoulder blades. He was just thirteen years old, but he was skilled in the use of all three weapons. Knowing by experience that he would have to wait at least an hour or two for the scout to finish his game, he placed the butt of his rifle on the ground between his feet so that the barrel rested against his thigh. He pulled out a book from his buckskin jacket pocket and began to read. The scout had taught him to read and had insisted that he read every day. By now Jack could read and understand books that the scout could barely comprehend, which made his adoptive father very proud.

Suddenly, there was a commotion at the table where the scout was playing, and a gambler shouted, "You're a cheat!" Jack quickly put the book back in his jacket and looked up to see one of the gamblers on his feet, facing his adoptive father. In a kind of slow motion, he watched them draw and saw his adoptive father fall with his gun still in its holster. Then his mind cleared, and he raced to the old scout and knelt down by him. He felt for a pulse, but there was none, for Ned Falcon was dead, shot through the heart. Jack felt his heart grow cold and still, for he had dearly loved this taciturn man who had taken him in at the tender age of two and had raised him like his own son. He had passed on all his skills as a tracker and hunter to Jack and had always treated Jack as an equal from the moment that Jack could lift and shoot his own rifle. Now Jack stood up slowly and faced the gambler, who had holstered his pistol and was telling the others, "That damn half-breed was cheating!"

"No, he wasn't," Jack said clearly, and the gambler and the other three men at the table turned to look at him. They saw a big-boned youngster with an angular face and keen blue eyes that now looked as cold and wild as a Kansas blizzard. "He didn't cheat," said Jack. "He didn't cheat because he never cheats." The gambler said in a disgusted voice, "Look kid, if you know the half-breed, just take him and go. He cheated and he got what he deserved." He was just about to sit back down when Jack said in a loud and clear voice, "You're a liar!" Everyone froze, and the gambler said in a bleak voice, "If you weren't still wet behind the ears, I would shoot you down like a dog for that!" Jack's hand hovered over his gun butt, and he said in a cold voice, "You're a liar! If you're not also a coward, then draw!" The gambler looked at the gun in Jack's waistband and then told the other men at the table, "You're witness to this. He's carrying, and he's called me out, so I got to put him down." Suddenly in a flash, his hand dropped for his gun, and a single shot rang out. With a surprised look on his face, the gambler crumpled to the ground, while Jack pushed his gun back into his waistband and lifted his rifle. "Anyone else got anything to say?" he asked.

Nobody said anything, and then the town Marshal walked in. He surveyed the scene and asked one of the men at the table, "Okay, Bill, so what happened here?" When he had heard everything, he turned to Jack and asked him, "You know that man, kid?" He was pointing to the old scout, and Jack said, "He was my adoptive father, and he never cheated in his whole life." The Marshal stared at Jack for a moment and then said, "Come with me, son." Seeing Jack hesitate and look down at the body of Ned Falcon, he added, "Don't you worry none, I'll get the undertaker to take care of the body." Jack walked out with the Marshal, and they went to his office. "Take a seat, son," said the Marshal as he sat down behind his desk. When Jack was seated, the Marshal said, "They call me Nate Dolan. What name do you go by?"

"Jack Donovan," Jack replied. "That was Ned Falcon, a scout and hunter." The Marshal asked him, "What happened to your folks, son? If you don't mind me asking." Jack looked at the Marshal and liked what he saw. "They were killed in a Ute raid on their wagon train. I was just two years old at the time, and Ned took me in, and I guess he kind of adopted me."

"How old are you, son?" the Marshal asked him in a kind voice. But Jack was by nature wary, and he didn't intend to be taken in and looked after by anyone else, so he said, "I'm turning sixteen this winter. Ned always told me that if anything happened to him, I was to go to his family in Colorado. He took me there a few times." The Marshal contemplated for a while, for he figured Jack to be way younger than sixteen. But then again, the Marshal knew this land, and he was a good judge of people. Coming to a decision, he looked up and said, "You're sure you can make it on your own?" Jack nodded and said softly, "He taught me all that he knew. I can track and hunt and use my rifle and pistol." The Marshal smiled and said, "Well now, you've proved that you can handle yourself, I'll give you that. That man you shot? He was known as a real hard man and fast with a gun." Jack just shrugged and said, "Ned taught me that there is always someone better somewhere. He used to say, 'Don't give yourself airs just because you are good with a gun, because there is always someone better.' He was a good man." The Marshal sighed and told him, "I'll take care of his burial, and I'll put that on his tombstone, 'He was a good man.' He taught you well." Jack thanked him and stood up. "I'd like to pay for his burial and his tombstone, and I'll be taking his outfit along with me," he said. The Marshal waved his hand and told him, "Son, I'll take care of it. Today I saw a youngster stand up for the honor of his adoptive father, and that's something you don't see every day." He stared at Jack for a moment and then said, "If you wouldn't mind some advice, I'd say always remember what Ned there told you. There'll always be someone better. You're going to use your gun again because you're good and you're fast, and so there'll always be a reason to; but just make sure you use it only for good. Don't ever cross the line, son, because I can tell you it's just not worth it."

The next day, Jack left town and drifted. He took on odd jobs at the towns he passed through, claiming to be sixteen years old. Most times he just lived off the land. It was a land of plenty, and with his skills, he never went hungry. He drifted through Utah and then turned south into New Mexico, and finally found himself in Texas. During the two years of his drifting, he got into a few gunfights and knife fights, but he soon earned a reputation in fistfights. At fourteen, he was a shade under six feet, with well-developed muscles from living off the land and from the hard work involved in the odd jobs he took on to put some money in his pocket. He chopped wood, felled trees, worked in mines, and did whatever was required to earn a living. In fistfights, he was up against rough, tough frontier men, and the fighting was dirty; knuckle, skull, and boots and no time out until one of the fighters was down for good. The type of fistfighting that Jack did was alien to most men in the country at that time, and it took his opponents by surprise. That was thanks to the training imparted to him at a young age by a Chinese cook.

When Jack was about ten years old, Ned Falcon took on a job of scouting and hunting meat for the railroad in an area of the Midwest where they were laying new track for a spur at the time. The cook for the railroad crew was Chinese, and he took a liking to the young boy who rarely spoke. He noticed the speed of the youngster's hands when Jack was practicing drawing his pistol, and he started teaching the boy an art of fighting that he told Jack was native to his country. It was bare hands fighting, but it was nothing like the knuckle and skull dirty fighting that was usual for that time and place in America. There was a kind of grace and fluidity in the way the Chinese moved. He concentrated on teaching Jack some moves that he said would help him take down a much bigger man without any trouble. Jack was a fast learner, and he absorbed the training sessions. He learned to use the knuckle of his middle finger in an extended position rather than just a closed fist. The Chinese cook taught him where the most vulnerable points of the human body lay. He taught him how to toughen the edge of his palms and to use it to hit. He showed Jack how much more effective it was than a closed fist. He taught him to use his feet as well in a fight, and soon Jack could deliver a kick to a height equaling his own. He also taught him what Jack thought of as a flying kick with the full force of his body behind it, where both his feet left the ground. He then taught Jack how to concentrate his mind and develop the center of his energy before exploding into action. Like everything else that Jack learned, he concentrated hard and practiced hard.

He was fifteen when he finally drifted into Texas, and in the town of Cedar Creek, he heard talk that the Double M ranch was hiring ranch hands for the annual roundup. He rode up to the ranch house in the evening when Ryan and Maria were sitting on the porch steps talking. Jack would later learn that the Double M brand was owned and run by Ryan McCullough, who was 32 at the time, and his wife Maria. They had two children, Bruce and Beth, eight years and six years old, respectively. Now he swung down from the saddle and walked up to Ryan, who had stood up and walked down the steps to meet him. "My name's Jack Donovan, and I heard in town that you were hiring hands for the roundup," said Jack. "You a cowboy, son?" asked Ryan. "No, Sir," said Jack. "I've done a lot of things to put food in my belly; I've taken care of horses and cows, worked in mines, cut trees, and done whatever was needed to be done." He added, "I'm a fast learner, Sir, and if you would be willing to teach me, I promise to work hard and do whatever the job takes." Ryan looked at him thoughtfully and then asked, "How old are you, son?" Jack said without hesitation, "Turned 18 this year, Sir."

Although Jack claimed to be 18, Ryan figured him to be much younger, although he didn't comment on it. He liked what he saw in the big-boned youngster standing in his yard, and he turned slightly to look at Maria, who gave him an almost imperceptible nod. "Work on a ranch is hard and dangerous, and it requires a lot of skill to handle the wild longhorns, son," Ryan said. "But if you're willing to work hard, then I guess I'll teach you. You have family somewhere, Jack?" Jack shrugged and replied, "No Sir, it's just me by my lonesome." Ryan said, "Come with me, and you can pick out a bunk in the bunkhouse for the night. We'll talk in the morning."

"If it's all the same to you," Jack said, "I'll just bed down under those trees over there." Ryan stared at him, and by way of explanation, Jack added, "I've been living off the land and sleeping under the stars for a few years now, and I guess I like it." Ryan shrugged and said, "Okay, but you'll have dinner with us." Jack walked to his horse and untied a burlap sack from the back of the saddle and brought it to Ryan. "I'll have that dinner if I can contribute," he said. Ryan opened the sack and saw a haunch of venison. He smiled at Jack and said, "Your contribution's welcome, son."

A few days later, after talking it over with Maria, Ryan told Jack that he would live with the family at the ranch house and not the bunkhouse, until he learned the job of being a cowhand. The excuse he gave was that it would be easier for him to teach Jack the skills of the trade, and also that Jack could help out in the house by lending a hand with the children. The truth was that there was something about the silent, independent youngster that struck a chord in both Maria and Ryan. Jack spent the entire day working and learning the ropes of handling cattle, but he still found time occasionally to contribute to the dinner table. Venison, jack rabbits, and once a bear!

Although Jack was a quick learner and soon became accepted by the ranch hands as one of them, he was always silent and withdrawn and would rarely speak unless spoken to. It was Maria who finally broke down the reserves of the youngster and learned the story of the wagon train and his adoptive father. Having never known a mother's love and affection, Jack soon worshipped the ground Maria walked on. She was the only one who could get Jack to open up and talk about his drifting life from the age of 13.

CHAPTER 3
LIGHTNING HANDS

It had been a little over a year since Jack had joined the Double M, and one day all the hands were at the western end of the ranch gathering the cattle for the annual roundup. As the cattle were gathered, they were driven to the holding ground, which was a large bench of good grassland with a watering hole, about a mile from the ranch house. On that particular day, Maria and two older cowhands were riding herd on the gathered cattle at the holding area. As they rode around the herd, singing to keep the animals calm, four men suddenly rode out from a grove of trees and approached the herd. Telling the two elderly cowboys to hold the herd, Maria rode out to meet the men. She stopped her horse when she was ten feet away and said, "Howdy, gentlemen, and what can I do for you? This is the Double M, and I would take it kindly if you would just ride around the herd so as not to spook them." While she was speaking, the men kept walking their horses towards her, and suddenly one of them dug in his spurs and his horse leapt forward. He slashed at Maria with the barrel of his gun, and she dropped like a stone from her horse and lay still. The other three men, meanwhile, continued riding fast towards the herd, and drawing their rifles they shot both the cowboys out of their saddles. Then all four of them began driving the cattle in a southern direction and were soon lost to sight in a cloud of dust.

Jack was at the ranch house as it was his turn to be the night rider and watch the herd during the night. Hearing the rifle shots, he picked up his rifle, and running out of the house, he jumped onto his horse without bothering to saddle up and rode bareback towards the herd. When he was still some distance away, he spotted the bodies lying on the ground and recognized the horse that Maria had been riding. Urging his horse on to greater speed, he rushed towards Maria. He reined in the galloping horse and, dropping down, he ran towards the motionless form of Maria. Gently, he felt for a pulse and heaved a sigh of relief when he found one. Taking the canteen from Maria's horse, he wet his bandana and gently sponged away the blood from her head to reveal a gash in her scalp that had already stopped bleeding. Rinsing out his bandana, he then gently bathed her face with clear water until she regained consciousness. "Can you ride?" he asked her. Maria looked wildly about and cried out when she saw the bodies of the two ranch hands. "Four men," she told Jack. "Four men! They knocked me out, and they must have rustled the herd. Please go and see how Tom and Bob are doing, Jack. I'm okay, just a bit dizzy from the blow to my head." Jack went over and found that both the old-timers were dead. He came back and told Maria, "I'm sorry, they're gone. Let me get you to the house first, and then I'll come back for them."

"No, Jack!" Maria cried. "I don't like to leave them lying in the open like that. We'll take them with us." Jack frowned but then relented, "Okay, I'll tie them to their horses, but you are not to move! Just lay here and rest until I've finished."

The sad cavalcade reached the house, and the children came running out together with the old cook. Jack carefully lifted

Maria from her saddle, carried her into the house and laid her on her bed. "Jack," Maria told him. "You must ride and tell Ryan what has happened. We just can't afford to lose those cattle; there were more than five hundred head in that herd." Jack stared at her for a moment and then said, "Bruce will ride and tell Ryan. I'm going after those rustlers before they ride clear of the border. They have a big head start right now." This was a different Jack, Maria realized as she stared at him. His face had hardened, and his blue eyes were cold. She cried, "Jack, you can't go after them alone; there are four of them!"

"You just rest up until Ryan gets here," was all he said in reply as he walked out and went to his room. He buckled on his gun belt and, out of habit, checked the action of his pistol before sliding it into the holster. Picking up his rifle again, he ran from the house, saddled up, and mounted his horse. Maria heard the sound of the running horse, and she told her son, "Go Bruce quickly and get your father!"

For the first two miles, Jack had no problem tracking the rustlers as they were pushing the herd as hard as they could to put distance between them and the ranch, and the trail was easy to follow. Then he came to a place where the tracks seemed to be all messed up, with the tracks of the horses and the cattle just all over the place. Jack sat in his saddle and contemplated the situation. His adoptive father had always drilled into him the value of contemplation. "When you seem to hit a dead end in tracking, don't run off in this direction and that direction searching for sign," he told Jack. "First study the situation, and then take a moment to contemplate. Put yourself in the shoes of the person or the mind of the animal that you are tracking, and think like they would. For that moment, you must become the hunted and not the hunter. Do that, and you will see your way clear." Jack had always followed the rule of the old scout, and many a time people had sworn that it was as though Jack could read the mind of the person he was tracking. Now he rode slowly forward until he came to the end of the morass of jumbled tracks, and then he looked around. He figured he knew what the rustlers were up to, but he intended to make sure all the same. He rode along the edge of the churned-up mud until he saw a bunch of tracks breaking away and heading southeast. He nodded in satisfaction, as it was proof that his theory was correct. The rustlers had split up the herd, and they were heading in two different directions. He figured two directions because it would require at least two men to drive even the split herd, and there being four rustlers, it figured that the herd was split into two. Not bothering to find where the other bunch of cattle had been headed, Jack followed the tracks of the herd he had found. It didn't take him long to find that he was right, because there were only the tracks of two horses riding with this herd.

He put his horse to the gallop, dividing his attention between the ground below and the land ahead. After another few miles of hard riding, he saw that far ahead the open grassland ended with a line of trees. He slowed his speed and kept a sharp lookout all around as he neared the tree line. The trees were not as dense as they appeared from a distance, and close up, they were actually well spread out. The tracks of the herd continued through the trees, but now Jack proceeded more slowly while carefully studying the land ahead as he moved. Suddenly, he heard the bellow of a steer, and the sound was very close. Dismounting, he hitched his horse to a tree, and taking his rifle he started off again on foot. After not more than ten yards, the land suddenly dipped, and Jack dropped to the ground and crawled the rest of the way until he could see over the lip of the slope. The incline was steep and then ended in flat land with very few trees and a small spring. He could see the herd settled in exhaustion near the spring and the two rustlers around a campfire making coffee.

From a rough count, he figured that this was the entire herd, which again proved that his assumption was right; they had split the herd and then joined up again later. It was approaching dusk now, and he strained his eyes to find the other two rustlers. He soon spotted them and realized that they were on sentry duty, with one of them watching the slope where he was and the other keeping a lookout opposite while riding around the herd. Jack patiently waited until the gloom of the gathering dusk deepened, and then he began moving forward on his belly. He had been trained by the scout who was half Sioux, and when he moved, he was as good as any Indian and disturbed neither stone nor grass to give his position away to the enemy. When he was within a stone's throw of the rustlers' camp, he lay flat behind a large bush and waited patiently for his opportunity to attack. The old scout had always told him, "The Indian is the greatest hunter and fighter the world will ever know because he understands the value of patience. A good hunter never becomes restless, never becomes impatient, never notices discomfort, but waits for his opportunity to strike; because he knows that if he waits long enough then the opportunity will arise, and when it does, he will always be ready."

Now Jack waited patiently just ten feet from the lookout, but the rustler was looking far up the slope and not at the ground near him, and he was oblivious to the danger lurking behind the bush. Suddenly one of the rustlers by the fire called out, "Hey, Nate, Josh, come over and have some coffee!" The lookout in front of Jack turned around and walked towards the fire. Immediately, Jack moved closer in a silent rush until he was hardly fifteen feet from the fire, hidden behind a tree. Slowly he stood up behind the tree, and with an economy of movement, he leant his rifle against the tree and checked that his gun was riding free in the holster. Peering around the tree, he saw that the fourth rustler had also come to the fire. Two were hunkered down by the fire and two were standing nearby. Silently, Jack moved around the tree and walked towards the fire, keeping the tree at his back so that he would not be silhouetted against the darkening sky. When he was about ten feet away, one of the rustlers spotted him and, squinting into the gloom, he said, "Hey, Cal, what the hell are you doing over there?" Jack tensed and then relaxed; he had called it wrong, there were five rustlers and the other bunch of cattle must have had three riders. But it was too late now to back off, and without losing a step, he continued forward another few feet and then said, "This is the end of the road for you. I'm taking the cattle back."

Cursing aloud, all four rustlers went for their guns. Three of them drew their pistols, but Jack was watching the fourth, who held a rifle in his right hand and was already swinging it up to shoot. Jack drew in a blur of speed, and fanning the hammer, four shots rang out. The first bullet took the rifle-toting rustler right between the eyes, and then the other three fell. While all three had managed to get their pistols clear of their holsters, none got a shot off. Before the last rustler fell, Jack had taken two quick steps back, half turned, and dropped prone to the ground, his eyes searching for the fifth rustler. The quick movement saved his life because the fifth rustler, who was off to his right, loosed off a shot immediately, and the bullet cut a groove on top of Jack's left shoulder as he was falling. Ignoring his wound, Jack took quick aim and fired, and the fifth rustler fell dead with a bullet in his heart. The flurry of shots disturbed the cattle, but it was over so fast that they quickly settled down again, being exhausted from the long, fast drive.

Jack cautiously walked over to check on all the rustlers, and he found only two alive, although just barely. He removed their guns and then went over to the fire. He checked his shoulder and found that although it was bleeding quite a bit, it was more a superficial wound about an inch deep. Bathing it with water from one of the rustlers' canteens, he folded his bandana into a thick pad and placed it over the wound. He then applied pressure to the pad to help stop the bleeding. Then he sat down and poured himself a cup of coffee. Suddenly there was a pounding of hooves, and a group of riders came over the rise and charged down towards the fire. Jack yelled, "Ryan!" and the leader of the group held up his hand, and the cavalcade slowed down and trotted their horses into the clearing. "Better get some men to the herd," Jack said. "The shooting made them a mite restless." Ryan gave the order and then walked up to Jack. "Are you okay, Jack?" he asked. "We were just about to give up because we couldn't see the tracks in the dark, when we heard the shooting and came charging in this direction." Jack shrugged and told him, "I'm okay, just a scratch on my shoulder. Two of them are still alive, and the fifth rustler is over there by the trees."

Ryan immediately pulled away the pad and inspected the wound. "That there's quite a scratch," he commented. He went to his horse, and from his saddlebags, he took out some strips of linen cloth and a pint of whiskey. He made Jack remove his shirt and said, "This will sting a mite, but it seems to cut infection." He poured some whiskey over the wound and then placed a clean pad on it and bandaged it tight. "That should hold until we get you to the ranch," he said. They tended to the two wounded rustlers, but one of them was gut shot and the other was shot through the lung, and both died soon after. Before dying, one of the rustlers asked Ryan, "Who is he? He took out the four of us after giving us fair warning and then turned and shot Cal, who was off to his right." Ryan shrugged and said, "He's just a kid, all of 16 years old, I believe." The dying rustler snorted, "Well, he's a kid with lightning hands, who is hell on wheels with that pistol, and he don't waste no bullets either!"

The word soon spread about how Jack singlehandedly went after the rustlers, shot down all five of them, and retrieved the cattle. The ranch hands accorded him space and respect as a real fighting man. About six months after the rustling incident, Jack and five of the younger ranch hands went to town one evening after drawing their wages. Jack was not much of a drinker, but he secretly enjoyed the company of these five cowboys, and they had become close friends, although they still called him 'Loudmouth Jack' because of his taciturnity; that was the way of the west! Billy, 18, and Clyde Hadden, 19, were brothers; Poco Pete was a 17-year-old half-Mexican, half-Apache tracker for the ranch; Will Dorsey, aged 17, was a local boy; and Jason Montana, who had just turned 18, was acknowledged as the fastest gun on the ranch until Jack came along.

The six young cowhands trooped into the First Chance Saloon and lined up at the bar. "Drinks!" yelled Billy Hadden to the barkeep. "Good whiskey, my friend! It's payday, and it's our night to howl!" Old Will Cook, the barkeep, knew the Double M boys, and he smiled and said, "Okay boys, the good stuff, and I'll keep it coming until you yell 'when'!" He knew that they weren't troublemakers, just young hellions shedding the grind of an entire month working on the ranch. He figured they were allowed to blow off some steam one night every month. The cowboys downed the first drink in a single swallow and then, picking up the second, they all turned around to survey the room. There was the usual sprinkling of locals with some travelling salesmen and a few professional gamblers. At a table in a corner sat three hard-faced strangers who looked like drifters, and at a table near them sat the town marshal, Bob King. He was nursing a drink and talking to his deputy, a young man of 20 who went by the name of Tom English. Bob King was well liked and respected by the town's citizens. He was also respected by the cowboys of the surrounding ranches, who figured that he always gave everyone a fair deal. If a cowhand took too much drink on payday and created a ruckus, he usually ended up for the remainder of the night in jail with a sore head and nothing more. The cowboys respected that because they knew that there were town marshals who would just as soon shoot a drunk troublemaker as knock him on the head.

Bob King lifted his hand to acknowledge the greetings of the cowboys and said, "How's the Double M doing these days, boys?" It was Jason Montana who answered, "Quiet and peaceful, Marshal, after Loudmouth here took care of those five rustlers." Will Dorsey said, "I guess the rustlers got the message that if they attack the Double M, then Loudmouth Jack would just talk them to death!" All the cowboys laughed and slapped each other on the back while Jack just shook his head with a wry smile and told the barkeep, "That's a good one. The next round's on me, I guess." Billy, Clyde, and Poco Pete walked over to a table where the house gambler sat and drew up chairs. "Let's go, Pat," Clyde told the gambler, Pat Delmont. "It's our night, and we're going to take the house for all it's worth. So stack 'em up and lay 'em out, and let's see what you got!" Pat just smiled and gathered up the cards to deal. The three strangers were talking softly to each other and glancing occasionally at Jack, who noticed them but acted unaware. In fact, he had seen their heads jerk up when the Marshal mentioned the Double M, and he had been keeping a wary eye on them since then. Without seeming to, he moved closer to Jason and Will and whispered, "Don't react, and don't make sudden moves, but I think something is going down with those three hombres over at the corner table. Will, make some excuse and leave the bar, but go around and stand by that window near their table. Jason, casually walk over to the Marshal's table and stay there. Keep your gun loose in its holster, and let's see where the chips fall. But take your cue from me and don't start nothing until we see what they intend."

It said much for the respect that Jack was held in by his friends that they didn't question him but just did as he asked. Will told the barkeep in a loud voice, "Hold my next round, Will. I'm a goin' to the outhouse but I'll be back." He walked out of the bar casually and, just as casually, Jason started walking over to the Marshal's table. As soon as Will exited the saloon and before Jason could reach the Marshal's table, the three strangers stood up and one of them swiftly walked over and put a gun to the back of the Marshal's head. The other two spread out facing the room and the bar with their hands on their guns. The one holding a gun to the Marshal's head said, "Now don't anyone make any funny moves or this will turn into a tragedy. We don't got no beef with no one here except for the Double M." One of the men facing the room looked at Jack and said, "We don't believe you killed those men in a fair fight, but now's your chance to prove us wrong. Draw and we'll see just how much of a liar you are."

As he spoke, he and his partner went for their guns and Jason Montana also started to draw, and Billy, Clyde, and Poco Pete began to get up. What happened next became a legend in the land. As they all went for their guns, three rolling shots rang out, so close that it sounded almost like a single shot. The man holding a gun on the Marshal went flying backwards with a bullet hole in the center of his forehead. The other two strangers had their guns only halfway out of their holsters when they were also thrown backwards, one with a bullet through his eye and the other with a bullet right through his mouth and out the back of his head. Jason's gun had just finished clearing his holster. For a moment following the roll of shots, everyone stayed frozen, except for Jack who was steadily replacing the spent cartridges in his pistol.

Then the room erupted; Will came running into the bar, Billy, Clyde, and Poco Pete, and indeed everyone else, jumped out of their chairs. Everyone was talking at once and Jason had a bemused expression on his face as he looked at his gun, which had just cleared his holster. "Stop!" the Marshal shouted and the voices died down. He walked over, bent down and looked at the three men, and then stood up and said in a casual tone, "Well Kid, they called you a liar and I guess you proved them wrong." He slowly shook his head and then added softly, "To tell you the truth, if I hadn't seen this I guess I wouldn't have believed it either." He walked over to Jack and shook his hand. "Son, you have lightning in them hands of yours. My only advice is, take care how you use them." He paused and then told Jack in a soft voice, "From now on you're a goin' to have to watch your back. There'll be more rannies like these who will want to buck you just to see how good you really are. What happened here today will spread like wildfire along the trails and gunslingers who want to make a name for themselves will come hunting you." Jason walked up to Jack and said, "I don't believe it! I figured myself to be fast, but I just about managed to get my gun out and the whole show was over." He slapped Jack on his back and shouted to the barkeep, "Drinks are on me, Will. Let's drink to the fastest gun in the west!"

After the shootout at the First Chance Saloon, life on the ranch went on as usual. It was a tough, hard life and it bred strong men and women. The work on a ranch was never-ending and it lasted from the break of dawn, sometimes earlier, to dusk and oftentimes later. There were cattle to be branded, watering holes to be dug and kept clean, moving the herd from pasture to pasture so that they did not eat the grass right to the ground, and a myriad of other things. Ryan was a smart rancher and he had laid out a field of alfalfa earlier on so that in the winter the herd had a good supply of hay and did not lose too much weight. Jack still lived at the ranch house and it was generally accepted by everyone that Jack had been unofficially adopted by Ryan and Maria.

Jack always tried to spend time with Bruce and Beth, teaching them tracking and the use and care of guns. He spoke to them late at night about the ways of the Indians and how on the frontier the word of a man was his bond, and if a man was known either as a cheat or a liar then no one would deal with him. "You must hate the Indians because they killed your parents," Bruce once told him. "No," Jack replied. "I don't hate them because that is just their way of life, hunting and raiding, and everyone is fair game to them except members of the tribe. Many people think that the Indian hates the white man and so they keep attacking the wagon trains and ranches, but it isn't so. An Apache raiding party will attack a Crow or Shoshone settlement just as soon as a wagon train." Bruce frowned and said, "But they are like devils, because they torture their prisoners!"

"To a white man it appears to be just torture," explained Jack. "Because only a white man who is a sadist and really cruel would do such a thing. But Indians do not torture their prisoners for fun; to them, it is a trial of strength and courage, and when a prisoner does not break under the torture then they praise him and respect him, although they still might kill him. For their way of life, strength, courage, and endurance are the qualities they need for survival and so they admire those who have that."

"But they take the scalps of the dead!" exclaimed Beth. "True," said Jack, "and sometimes of the living as well! They call it counting coup and the warrior with the most number of scalps is treated with great respect in the tribe. But do you know that if they respect a person as being brave and courageous in a fight, then they will not scalp him? They leave him his scalp as a mark of honor."

"But I have heard stories that some settlers and ranchers who tried to be nice to them and gave them food and gifts were murdered by them," said Bruce in a puzzled voice. Jack laughed and then explained, "That is really what is called a clash of civilizations. The white man thinks that by gifting an Indian food and things he will be regarded as a generous and good man, because that is the way white people are taught. But to an Indian, it is a sign of weakness and fear, which are attributes that he despises, so he kills them because he thinks they are cowards."

One night Bruce asked Jack, "You read almost every night. Did you go to a school?" Jack smiled and then said seriously,

"The best school is the school of life and it is all around you if you pay attention and study it. The scout who adopted me taught me how to live off the land and how to protect myself, but he also taught me how to read and it was a strict rule that I read at least two pages every day before going to sleep. No matter how tired I was!" Beth frowned and asked, "But if he taught you how to survive off the land, why would he insist on you reading a book? What good is that?" Jack sat up and said, "He told me, 'I can teach you how to live off this land and how to survive even in the desert, but there is a whole world out there and you will find them in books.' So he made me read and it became a kind-a habit, and truth to tell it does teach you a lot about life and people and the world around us." Bruce immediately said, "I am also going to read at least two pages every day before I sleep." Beth chimed in, "Me too!" Jack smiled and said, "Good for you, Bruce, and good for you, Beth. You won't regret it, I promise!"

Jack had completed two years on the ranch, and to celebrate that event, Jason Montana and Poco Pete took him into town with Ryan's blessings. Billy was laid up with an injured leg; a steer had fallen on it, and Clyde stayed back to keep him company. Will Dorsey had chores to do, so Jason, Poco Pete, and Jack rode into town. They went to their favorite watering hole, the First Chance Saloon, and Jason told the barkeep, "It's an anniversary! Loudmouth here has completed two years with us, so keep the drinks coming!" Two strangers were sitting at a table and one of them got up and came to the bar. He slapped Jack on the shoulder and said, "Well, congratulations, kid! Let's drink to that anniversary, I'm buying!" Jack took two steps away from the stranger and said, "No thanks, Mister, I'm not much of a drinker." The forced half-smile on the stranger's face faded away and he snarled, "Think you're too good to drink with me, huh? That's an insult! Are you insulting me, kid?"

While he was speaking, his hand hovered above his gun butt,

but if he intended to confuse Jack and push him into making a mistake, then he was about to learn different. Jack stared at him calmly and said, "You've been reading too many dime novels, Mister. Let me see now, I'm supposed to say that I'm not insulting you, and then you will say that I'm calling you a liar and you'll draw your gun immediately, thinking that you will catch me unprepared. After killing me, you will justify your sly move by claiming that I called you a liar and you were defending your honor. Have I got it right so far?" The stranger by now had a very confused look on his face, and shaking his head, he snarled, "I'm Laredo Smith and..." Before he could complete his sentence, Jack held up his left hand to stop him and said, "Well, Laredo, that's where you should have stayed. I'm saying that you are a liar and a cheat and a coward and a cheap four-flusher who thinks he is a gunman, so draw!" As Jack was speaking, he casually moved closer to Laredo Smith and as he said 'draw!' Laredo found himself looking into the bore of Jack's pistol which was inches away from his face. His eyes widened and his face turned deathly pale. He had never seen Jack draw his gun; it was just there, right in his face! Jason Montana drawled, "I've got his friend covered, Jack."

Jack took Laredo's gun from its holster and smacked him across the face with the barrel. Laredo staggered back and spat out a tooth and his mouth filled with blood. Jack turned and placed his gun and Laredo's gun on the bar and told Poco Pete, "Keep an eye on that will you; I aim to see just how tough ole Laredo here is." Pete looked at him and saw a Jack he had not seen before. There was a bleakness and a hardness to his face and his blue eyes were cold and empty; he looked suddenly ten years older. Jack walked up to Laredo and unleashed a whipping right cross to the chin, and when Laredo staggered back he caught hold of him and whipped a left into his stomach. As Laredo doubled over, he caught Jack's right hook to the face that broke his nose and sent him staggering back again. Jack then proceeded to give him a scientific beating that left him moaning and broken on the floor when he was finished. Laredo never got the chance to land even a single punch. Jack went to the bar and retrieved his gun and slid it into his holster. He gave Laredo's gun to the barkeep and said, "Keep it as a souvenir." He walked over to the other man and said, "You want to take up where ole Laredo left off?" The man raised his hands and backed off, saying, "No Mister, I ain't got nothing to do with this." Jack stared at him for a moment and then said, "Take your partner and leave town right now. And spread the word that if anyone else wants a piece of me they'll have to find me 'cause I'm leaving town myself and I don't intend to be back here anytime soon."

CHAPTER 4
DRIFTING

RYAN AND MARIA TRIED THEIR BEST TO DISSUADE Jack from leaving. "I've heard of this Laredo Smith," said Ryan. "He is supposed to be real fast with a gun, and you sent him packing without a shootout. Now others will think twice about bracing you, so you don't really have to leave, Jack." Maria said, "Jack, even if these gunfighters come hunting you, at least here you will have the ranch hands to back you up. You're their hero now, and they'll die for you if necessary! You know that."

Jack sighed and told her, "Yes, I do know that, and it is because of that that I have decided to drift. Someday they'll go into town without me, and if they run into a gunman who badmouths me, then their pride would make them defend my honor and someone could die. I can't live with that, Maria. Once the word spreads that I have left town, these glory-hunting gunslingers won't bother to come here searching for me." Ryan grunted and said, "I guess I just don't like the idea of you drifting again, Jack." Jack shrugged and told him, "Neither do I, but this I've got to do, as there's no other way." He hesitated and then said, "That old scout, Ned Falcon, who took me under his wing and cared for me, was the only family I had ever known, until I came over here." He fidgeted a bit and looked embarrassed, but then said, "You folks took me in and have been a real family to me, and that is something I will never forget." He looked at Maria and said, "I have never known a mother's care and love, but you kind-a took care of that, and I'm sure grateful to have known you. If ever you folks need my help, just send the word along the trails, and I'll come a-running as soon as the word reaches me."

Jack took Bruce and Beth on a hunting trip for a week with Maria's permission. Bruce was mounted, and Beth rode with Jack. They left the ranch far behind and rode up into the hills. He pointed out medicinal plants to them and told them what the Indians used them for. They all wore moccasins, and he taught them how to walk silently by feeling the ground beneath their feet before planting their weight, so that no stone rolled nor dry stick broke. He would stop many a time and point out the tracks of deer, mountain lion, rabbit, and a host of other animals. He made them study the tracks carefully, and when they came across a similar track, he would ask them to name the animal. He taught them how to build a smokeless fire and how to heat water in a vessel made out of bark. Bruce was thrilled and absorbed everything that Jack taught them. He asked Jack, "Why doesn't the fire burn the bark?" Jack explained, "As long as the fire is below the level of water in the bark, the heat of the fire is absorbed by the water, and so the bark does not burn." He made the fire bigger, and immediately the bark went up in flames.

One day they tracked a mountain lion, with Bruce and Beth leading the way and doing the tracking. Suddenly they heard a squealing in the brush, and Bruce found a pair of lion cubs. Beth picked them up and was playing with them when Jack said, "Beth, put them cubs down, and you and Bruce come away from there right now!" The harsh tone of Jack's voice made them obey immediately, but when they withdrew with Jack to a safe distance, Beth cried, "Why couldn't I play with them? They are so cute, and they are harmless!" Jack shushed her and said, "Wait and watch. Sure, they're cute and harmless, but their mother isn't!" Within a few minutes, they spotted the mother lioness slinking through the brush to her cubs. Jack told them, "A lioness doesn't abandon her cubs, so when you see some cubs all alone, don't get fooled, because the mother isn't far away. She will always come back for them unless she is dead." He showed them how to build a shelter with tree boughs by weaving the slender branches together. The nights were cold, and they dug shallow pits in the sand and slept in them. "The sand will retain the heat of the day for quite a while," Jack told them. "Besides, the sand protects you from the cold wind, and so you can stay warmer in that shallow pit for the night."

At the end of the trip, he said his goodbyes to Bruce and Beth and told Bruce, "Remember whatever I have taught you, kid. You may not become real fast with a gun, but always remember to make the first shot count. Many a fast gun concentrates so much on the fast draw that he misses that first shot and loses out to a slower but calmer man who never misses that first shot." He told Beth, "You're pretty good with a rifle, so keep practicing. This is a rugged land, and it is especially tough on women, so the best thing to do is for you to become tough." He added, "At least, according to me." Beth hugged him hard and cried a lot. She was almost 8 years old now, and Jack had spent a lot of time teaching her, along with Bruce.

Jack left the Double M and drifted into New Mexico Territory. One day, he rode into the town of San Miguel and walked into the nearest saloon for something to eat. He was finishing the last of his bread and chilli beans when a man at the bar asked him, "Ain't you the kid who beat up Laredo Smith? You sure fit the description." Jack had noticed the man and four others talking together with casual glances in his direction. He had pegged them for gunmen and knew there would be trouble, but he was hungry, and so he continued eating. Now he mopped up the last of the beans with the last piece of bread and chewed slowly while he wiped his hand on his jeans. "I'm talking to you, kid!" the man said, raising his voice, which made all the other men in the room look at him. Jack swallowed his food and slowly stood up. He said mildly, "And if I am?" The man said, "If you are, then you are also the kid who supposedly took down five rustlers." Jack again asked, "And if I am?" The man took a step forward, and his hand was near his gun when he said, "Maybe I aim to see if the stories are true!" Jack said, "You alone or together with your four pards over there?" The gunman's eyes shifted as he realized that Jack was aware that there were five of them. He snarled, "Those so-called rustlers that you killed were friends of ours, and we think that you bushwhacked them." Jack gave him a cold smile and said, "So you figured that it would take five of you to handle a cowardly bushwhacker?" All five were now facing Jack, and one of them said, "That's enough talking!" He went for his gun, and so did the rest of them. Jack palmed his gun, and three shots rang out, and three men fell. The other two got off a shot each, and Jack felt a blow to his side, and a bullet singed his ear, but he was already taking two quick steps to his right, and he shot twice more, and the remaining two men crumpled to the ground. There was a heavy silence in the saloon after the shooting stopped, and then the room erupted with everyone talking at the same time. "Did you see that? He got all five!"

"I never saw his hand move!"

"He was fanning the hammer, but it was so fast that it was just a blur!"

"I heard tell that they call him Lightning Hands!"

"He's lightning all right!"

Ignoring all the talk, Jack replaced the spent bullets in his gun, and holstering it, he walked out of the saloon without speaking. Mounting his horse, he rode out of town and stopped only after he had ridden for more than a mile. Then he dismounted and tended to his wound. The bullet had cut a furrow in his side, but it was a superficial wound, and he dabbed it with whiskey and bound it up before continuing on his way. He was just seventeen years old.

The thought was in his mind that he needed to go to a place where no one knew him. He never took pleasure in gunfights, and if possible, he wanted to avoid trouble. As he neared Arizona, he heard talk in saloons of a gold rush that was beginning, and that boom towns were flourishing along the Gila River. He had worked in mines before, and a boom town was usually filled with strangers and drifters, so he decided to head over there. Besides, he figured he could also earn some eating money and maybe a stake for the future.

He rode into the boom town of Gila City and found the town bustling with people and activity. Single large rooms built with rough-hewn logs, tents, and dugouts had sprung up all around the town, and any number of stores in town sold mining equipment. The saloons outnumbered all the other buildings. Jack soon discovered that mostly placer mining was being done and that the gold haul was quite good in places. He soon found an unclaimed area and staked out a site for himself. He went to town to stock up on food, ammunition, and mining equipment. Having bought all he needed, he walked into the Placer Gold Saloon and ordered a whiskey. Standing at the crowded bar, he was next to a man who looked like a miner but who was drinking with a gloomy expression on his face. The miner finished his whiskey and looked up and caught Jack's eye. "Friend," he said, "you don't know me, and I don't know you, but I'd admire if you would buy me a drink to drown my sorrows. I will repay you when I can. But I must warn you that that may be some time away." Jack said with a half-smile, "You look like a hard-working miner, and I hear tell that folks are making good money from placer mining. So why the sorrow, if you don't mind me asking?" The man said, "Buy me a drink, friend, and I'll tell you." Jack liked the cut of the man, so he bought him a drink. Downing the drink, the man stuck out his hand. "I'm Bill Nevers," he said. "I worked hard and took out a pile of gold this past month, and then I was robbed. That's the reason for my sorrow."

Jack told him, "I'm Jack Donovan and I intend to do some placer mining myself." Bill said eagerly, "I'll work for you for wages! Until I save up enough to buy my own outfit again. Those thieves held me at the point of a gun, and not satisfied with taking my gold, they also stole my outfit, my horse, and everything I owned. Then they knocked me senseless and left me for dead!" Jack said, "I'll tell you what. I've got all the equipment we'll need. We work as equal partners with you doing most of the mining while I take care of the security. Anyone tries to rob us, I'll deal with them." Bill Nevers took a second look at Jack. It was the way he had said that he would deal with any thieves that impressed Bill. There wasn't a trace of boasting in the way that he spoke, it was just said as a statement of fact. Bill took in the low-slung gun and the rifle that seemed an extension of this man's left hand, and he suddenly stuck out his hand. "You've got a deal, partner," he said. "But I must warn you that here the thieves don't come only at night, they come at any time. There's no law worth the name around here, and it's every man for himself." Jack shrugged and said, "You concentrate on the gold and I'll take care of the rest."

CHAPTER 5
GILA CITY

THEY PUT UP A TENT ON THE STAKED SITE AND BILL Nevers did wet panning and dry panning, and every day he came up with a cache of gold. Some days it was very little, and some days it was a good amount. Jack soon caught on to the knack of panning and did his share of the work, but always with his gun on his hip and his rifle within arm's reach. Bill's rifle was also never far away from him. After a week of hard work, Bill hefted the small poke of gold and told Jack, "Maybe we should cash this in before we get robbed and put the money in a bank, then we can continue to work." Jack shook his head and said, "No, we'll wait until we have enough to be worth going to a bank. Besides, they could waylay us on the way to town even now. They know we are finding gold." Bill looked surprised and asked him, "What makes you say that?" Jack shrugged and explained, "I figure these bandits are watching all the miners from them hills with telescopes. I've seen the sun reflect off glass many times this week." Bill's face turned red and he exclaimed, "So that's how they knew when to attack me!" Jack said, "Don't worry about it. Let's just keep working, and when we have a good enough stake they'll come to us here."

Two more miners were attacked and robbed the following week, and then the robbers came to Jack's claim. Maybe they didn't like the look of Jack because they were wary when they came. They came in the night, and they came silently; or so they assumed. Jack was always a light sleeper, and like any man who lived alone in the forests or the mountains, he always came awake instantly alert and reaching for his gun. His mind was attuned to the normal sounds of the night wherever he slept, but any sound that was not natural would wake him instantly. Now he came awake and he listened for the sound that had disturbed his sleep. The night was silent, and then it came again; the scuff of a boot on sand and the rolling of a small stone. He was instantly on his feet and shook Bill awake with a whispered warning. Then he glided away and lay down behind the low ramparts that they had built all around their camp.

There were six attackers, and the silence of the camp reassured them that this would be a surprise attack. When they were a few feet away from the rampart of sand, they opened fire at what seemed to be the forms of two men sleeping. But that was just two made-up pallets that Jack always placed in the open with bunched-up clothes covered by a blanket to make it appear like a man sleeping. The roll of gunshots stopped and the attackers took a step forward, peering into the darkness at the two forms that they had just shot up. That was when Jack, rising up on one knee, opened fire with his Colt revolving rifle and each shot took down an attacker. It was over in less than a minute, and Jack cautiously arose and approached the fallen attackers. Kicking away their guns, he bent and checked for life, and found that two were still in the land of the living. He called out softly, "Bill, come here and help me get these two bandits into the camp."

They dragged the men inside the camp, and with an oil lamp they examined the wounds. One man was gut-shot and wouldn't make it, but the other would, although he was shot through the chest. The bullet had entered just below his shoulder and had exited cleanly. They bound up his wound, by which time he had regained consciousness. Jack told him, "Your sidekicks are dead and this one here is gut-shot and won't make it through the night. If you want to live, you're going to tell me where your camp is and how many more men are out there."

"Go to hell," the bandit snarled. "You first," said Jack, pressing down on his wound. The bandit groaned and then snarled again, "You do what you want, but I ain't talking!" Jack said mildly, "I've lived among the Sioux and the Apache, and I know all the tricks that they have to break a man down to a bawling child." He turned to Bill and said, "Personally, I think that the Apache has it over the Sioux when it comes to breaking a man. They hang a man from his ankles and light a fire under his head. Now, the fire doesn't actually reach his head, so he doesn't just burn up. Instead, the flame is built so that it reaches to within a few inches of his head and slowly but steadily cooks his brain until it leaks out of his ears."

He paused as though he was contemplating the picture and then said casually, "Of course, I've never seen a man who lasted that long. It usually takes just about three minutes and then the man is bawling and screaming his head off." He looked around and said, "I think those tent poles should take his weight. Build a fire under them, Bill, and then help me to tote this gent over there and we'll hang him from his ankles." He then began lashing the man's arms to his body and tying his feet together. The matter-of-fact way that Jack spoke and the way he went about trussing him up without asking any further questions finally broke the man and he said, "Now look here, you're a white man and white men don't do things the Indian way." Jack shrugged and said, "Well, we'll soon find out, won't we? How's that fire coming, Bill?" He picked up the man's bound legs and began to drag him over to the fire, and the man yelled, "Please Mister, please, don't do it! I'll tell you what you want to know."

Jack simply said, "I'm waiting, and I'm not a patient man." The man said, "You see that odd-shaped hump of rock just above the tree line? The camp is about twenty feet right behind that rock. There are about ten men there, I would reckon." Jack looked at Bill and asked, "What do you think, Bill? Think he's telling the truth?" Bill gave the man a thoughtful look and then said, "I dunno, Jack, maybe he is and maybe he isn't. Tell you what though. Let's just hang him over the fire anyway and see if he changes his story." The man yelled, "No, no, please Mister, I'm telling you the truth. There shouldn't be more than ten men there now!" Jack smiled at Bill and then said, "I guess he's telling the truth. But keep him here all trussed up like he is, and I'll go check out if he's telling the truth." He bent over the bandit and said, "If you're lying and I don't come back, then my friend here is going to roast you, so for your sake, I hope you're telling the truth." The man almost whimpered, "I'm telling the truth, Mister, believe me. But how are you going to deal with ten men on your lonesome? You won't come back and this gent here will then roast me!" Jack shrugged and said, "Don't worry about it, he don't know the ways of the Indian." With that, Jack left the camp, and without taking his horse, he broke into a loping run with the rifle in his hands and an extra pistol shoved into his waistband. Watching Jack run, the man looked at Bill and asked, "What's he mean by you don't know the ways of the Indian?" Bill didn't know either, but he simply looked wise and stayed silent.

 Jack reached the rock and slowed down, and then began to advance more cautiously. He came around the rock, crouched low to the ground, and immediately he saw the campfire. He began crawling silently until he was within ten yards of the fire, and he counted exactly ten men. Some were standing and some were sitting around drinking coffee and eating. Leaving his rifle, he drew the extra pistol from his waistband and slowly rose to his feet and said conversationally, "I hear you men are looking to rob some more gold from the miners." Cursing, the men dropped their coffee mugs and lunged to their feet, drawing their guns. Jack's gun began speaking with Jack fanning the hammer. He dropped the empty gun and then drew his pistol from his holster and continued firing. It was over in seconds, and none of the men were left standing. Jack had fired four fast shots and then took two steps to the right and fired twice more before dropping the extra pistol and drawing his six-gun from his holster. He dropped to one knee and fired another four shots. Fanning the hammer was the fastest way to empty a six-gun, but it took a lot of practice to be accurate while doing so. Jack's shooting was always accurate, and he did not waste bullets.

Many of the men got their guns out and fired off a few shots, but most of the shots went wild. One shot grazed the side of Jack's left arm, and another sent his hat spinning, but that was the closest they got. It must be said that many a man could fan a six-gun as fast as Jack, but very few could do so with Jack's accuracy. Not bothering to check on the men, Jack turned around and headed back to his camp on the run. When he was about halfway back, there was the report of a rifle and Jack felt a blow to the side of his body. He spun around and threw himself sideways to the ground and then rolled over again as another shot sounded and the bullet kicked up dirt where he had first fallen before rolling over. Jack rolled back to where the bullet had hit the ground and another bullet just missed him by a whisker. But he had spotted the shooter now, who was on one knee halfway down the slope and was in the act of reloading his rifle. Taking quick aim, Jack fired his rifle and the shooter seemed to crumple in slow motion and then rolled down the slope for about ten feet and lay still.

Jack pulled out his shirt and checked his wound, which was starting to bleed a lot. The bullet had entered his side just above his hip without hitting the bone, and Jack put his hand around his back and felt for an exit wound. He sighed when he realized that the bullet had gone clean through. Taking out his bowie knife, he cut strips from his shirt and plugged the entry and exit holes as best he could. Then he took his bandana and carefully tied it tightly around his body to hold the plugs in place, and then slowly walked back to his camp. He walked straight to the fire, and sitting down, he told Bill, "I'm hit and I need a bit of help." He put the blade of his bowie knife in the fire and then carefully removed his bandana. "When the knife is really hot," he told Bill, "I need you to pull out these plugs and cauterize the wound on both sides. But first, just pass me my saddlebags." Bill didn't waste time asking what had happened but brought Jack's saddlebags to him immediately. Jack rummaged in the bag and brought out a leather poke, which he opened and took out some leaves and some bark. He placed the bark carefully aside, and then, taking out a small cup and a wooden pestle, he pounded the leaves with some water into a poultice. He took out some linen strips and made two pads, by which time the knife blade was starting to turn red. "Listen carefully, Bill," he said. "I'm going to put this poultice on both these pads. As soon as you've cauterized the wound, you need to place these pads on both ends with the poultice directly on the wound. Then tie this linen strip around my waist tightly to hold the pads in place." He placed the long strip on the ground and lay on it on his side with his wounded side being on top. Bill took the knife and did as Jack had instructed. Other than a hissing sound through clenched teeth when the hot knife was applied to the wound, Jack was silent throughout the operation. After he was satisfied that the wound was bound up nicely, he told Bill, "Shred some jerky into the pot, add this bark, and boil it for some time." Bill had placed his saddle near him, and using that as a pillow, Jack stretched out on the ground.

While the water was boiling, Bill asked, "So what happened? Heard a lot of shots at first and then after some time some more closer to camp. Were you bushwhacked, Jack?" Jack said, "There were ten men at the camp just like this yahoo claimed, but when I was halfway back here, I was shot by a man who was about halfway up the slope. He wasn't there when I went up, so he must have been returning to the camp when he heard the shooting, and then seeing me, he shot me from the back."

"You get him?" Bill asked. Jack said, "He won't be shooting anyone else in the back, and before you ask, those ten men won't be robbing anyone else either." The wounded bandit was lying some feet away, and now he said, "You got them all? What are you, Mister? Lightning hands?" Bill said, "You better just shut up, the fire is still burning!" But the bandit said, "I saw him shooting at us, and I swear I never saw anyone's hands move so fast!" Turning to Jack, Bill said, "What's with the poultice and the bark?" Jack explained, "The Indians use them for wounds. The poultice seems to help with healing and preventing infection, while the bark is good for reducing the inflammation of the wound and for the pain."

When the jerky and bark had boiled enough, Jack drank some of the broth and put by the remainder for later. Bill asked him, "What do we do with this bandit? His wound isn't much and he will be up within a few hours, by morning I reckon." Jack pondered for a moment and then said, "Tell you what. I won't be able to work for at least two days or even three. So I'll stand guard while you put him to work. Hobble his legs with a two-foot strip of rawhide so he can't run." The bandit snorted, "Like hell I will! I ain't doing no work for you!" Jack said mildly, "Was I you, I'd work. But you do what you want. What name do you go by anyway?" The bandit scowled and said, "Nate Downey. Why do you want to know?" Jack told him, "Just need to know what to put on your tombstone. Bill, tie him to those tent poles and put him over the fire." He told the bandit, "See, if I didn't come back, Bill here wouldn't know how to do this right. But now I'm here to show him how, and I'm betting that in two minutes flat you'll be yelling and pleading to work for us." The bandit stared at him and then said, "I believe you would actually do it too! Okay, okay, I'll work!"

It took a week before Jack's wound had healed sufficiently for him to move around freely, by which time they had a sizeable amount of gold, and Jack told Bill that they would ride into town and split the take. Jack set Nate Downey free, and giving him a small amount of gold, he told him, "You've worked for this, so it's yours. Maybe now you'll figure that it's better to work than to rob." Nate looked at Jack and said, "Mister, you're a square shooter, so I'll tell you this. I'm gonna try my best to earn my living honestly from now on." They rode into town and took the gold to the bank. Jack found himself with five hundred dollars, which was a small fortune at the time, and he told Bill, "I got to be moving on, but it was a pleasure working with you. Maybe we'll meet again sometime down the trail." When they parted ways, Jack had just turned eighteen.

CHAPTER 6
THE SONORAN DESERT

JACK DRIFTED INTO MEXICO JUST TO SEE THE country. He had money in his pocket and did not need to work, so he rode slowly and drank in the flavor of the land. He spent his nights sleeping in the open under the stars and only went into a town when he needed supplies. Most of the land was desert, but Jack liked the loneliness and silence of the desert, and he knew how to survive in it. He admired the soaring majesty of a mesa and even a butte, the tall somber silhouette of a saguaro against a darkening sky, and the plummeting dive of the desert hawk. He was deep into Sonora when he visited a small pueblo for some food supplies and ammunition. He was so tanned by the desert sun that he could easily pass as a Mexican. After stocking up on his supplies, he visited a cantina for a drink and some food. After eating his own cooking for so long, he always relished eating in a cantina on his rare visits to civilization. He was eating tortillas with chilli beans when there was a commotion outside, and then four soldiers came in, dragging a young Yaqui girl with them. She had a rope around her neck with the end being held tight by one of the soldiers.

They sat down at a table, and the soldier who seemed to be

in charge held the girl tightly on his knee. Slapping the tabletop, he shouted, "Hola! Bring us some tequila and make sure it's good!" The cantina owner pushed his wife into the back room and then came and put a bottle with four glasses on the table. It was obvious that he was terrified, and he bowed and asked, "Can I get the Capitan something to eat? Our tortillas and chilli beans are excellent." The soldier grunted assent as he poured the tequila into a glass and downed the drink in one gulp. Jack saw the other customers slowly leave the room, and he figured these soldiers were bad news to the locals. Suddenly, the captain, who had the girl on his knee, noticed Jack. He stared more closely at Jack and then said, "You are not Mexicano, my friend. You are gringo! What brings you to this Godforsaken place?" Jack shrugged and continued eating. "I like the desert and I wanted to see your country," he said. The captain laughed and said, "Well gringo, if you like the desert, then you will surely like this desert flower!" He began fondling the girl openly, but the girl managed to get a hand free and slapped him hard across his face. He roared in rage and began hitting the girl. The captain had his hand raised to strike the girl again when Jack spoke. "I wouldn't do that if I were you," he said mildly.

The captain froze with his hand raised, and then turned his head slowly to look at Jack. "What was that you said, gringo?" he asked in a hard voice. The cantina owner came hurrying over with two plates of tortillas and chilli beans, and he said placatingly, "He's a gringo, Capitan, and he doesn't know our ways. Here, taste this food and I promise you will enjoy it." The captain struck the plates to the ground and stood up, still holding the girl tightly with one hand. The other three soldiers also stood up, and they held their rifles at the ready, waiting for their captain's orders. "I asked you, gringo, what did you say?" the captain shouted. Jack wiped his hand on a cloth and then rubbed it on his jeans. He had been eating with his right hand while his left hand was under the table. The soldiers could not see that his left hand held his rifle. Now his right hand rested on his thigh after he had rubbed it clean on his jeans. He looked at the captain and said mildly, "I said, I wouldn't do that if I were you. That's no way to treat a girl." The captain laughed, "Girl? This little Yaqui snake killed two of my men! Knifed them!" Jack shrugged, "Maybe they were treating her like you are now?" The captain looked puzzled, "Of course they were! They were trying to have a little fun with her! Her people ambushed my patrol and left four of my men dead before vanishing into the desert. We came across a camp later on, and this girl was there along with her parents. We killed them and took her captive, which was when she knifed two of my men who were having a little fun with her." Jack said softly, "Good for her!"

"What was that, gringo?" shouted the captain. "Are you looking to die here? If I say the word, my men will cut you down where you sit!" Jack still looked relaxed, and he again spoke softly and said, "Was I you, I would cut her loose and let her return to her people. You killed her parents, so why do you need her?" The captain shouted, "You are a fool, gringo! I will rape her and then all my men will rape her, and finally we will torture her and kill her. Then we will throw her body in the desert as a warning to her people! That is the only language these savages understand!"

"I don't think I can allow that to happen," said Jack in a conversational tone.

It took a moment for Jack's words to sink in, and then the captain snarled, "Kill him!" The other three soldiers could not understand English, and they were looking confused at the talk that was taking place. When their captain shouted, they first looked at him and then turned back to Jack, raising their rifles to shoot. But that was too long a reaction time when dealing with someone like Jack. He shot one of them with his rifle from under the table, and then he palmed his six-gun and triggered three fast shots that took out the other two soldiers and the captain. The captain still held the rope in his hands, and when he fell the girl fell with him, and the noose tightened around her throat. She struggled to free herself, and Jack ran over and removed the noose. The cantina owner came running and told Jack, "Senor, you have killed Capitan Cortez. He has many men under his command, and he comes from an influential family. They will hunt you down, senor! Your only hope is to run for the border!" Jack saw that the man was serious, and he said, "That seems like a good idea. I guess I'll be moving now." The cantina owner was talking to the girl, and now he told Jack, "Take her with you, senor. She knows the desert, and her people are there. She can help you to get to the border." Jack looked at the girl and said, "Well, I'll get her to her people, and then I'll make my own way to the border."

He turned around and headed for the door, and the girl followed him out. He saw the horses of the soldiers, and he quickly stripped the saddles from three of them and roped them together, but he held on to the canteens. They rode hard and fast, leading the three spare horses for almost ten miles, and then they were right in the middle of the desert. Jack held up his hand, and they stopped. Taking a canteen and his bandana, he rinsed out the mouths of the horses. Then, pouring some water in his hat, he let each horse drink a little. Quickly stripping the saddles from their horses, he transferred them to two of the other horses. "They'll ride easier without our weight," he said. Looking at the girl, he smiled and said, "I guess communicating is going to be a problem. I don't know Yaqui and you..." Before he could complete his sentence, the girl said, "I know English. Missionary teach me when I young." Jack was surprised, but all he said was, "Well, let's mount up. If you know where your people are, just point the way!"

They rode through the heat of the day, and every now and then Jack would stand up in his stirrups and look around to see if he could spot any pursuers. The last time he did so, there was a heat haze all around, and it was hot as hell, but Jack shaded his eyes and scanned the land all around. Suddenly, he stiffened in the saddle, and pointing, he told the girl, "Look over there, that's dust. It could be the soldiers have found our trail." The girl was agitated and said, "We must move. Fast. My people are still many miles distant." But instead of starting his horse, Jack dismounted and started rummaging in his saddlebags.

"What you do?" the girl cried. "Must ride fast!"

Ignoring her, Jack removed a burlap sack and some rawhide strips from his saddlebags. He told the girl, "Wait! Come and help me." He took out his Bowie knife and cut the sack into strips. Then he showed the girl how to tie the strips of burlap around the horses' hooves with the rawhide strips. The girl immediately understood, and together they completed the task in a short time. The girl smiled and said, "Smart! I am called Dyani. It means a deer because I am fleet of foot." Jack also smiled, "I'm Jack. I think I'll just call you Dani. Let's ride!"

As they rode, Jack explained, "The wind is picking up, and the sacking will not leave much of a trail. The wind will wipe out whatever is there." Dani nodded and said, "I understand. Smart!"

They rode fast for another ten miles, and then Jack called a halt near a large outcropping of rock which was almost a small hill. Leading the horses, they carefully picked their way up through the broken rocks and saguaro cactus. Crossing the crest of the hill, they found a small plateau shaded by giant cacti, and there they tethered the horses and lay down to rest. From time to time, Jack would crawl up to the top and look all around to see if they were being followed. The third time he did this, he saw a group of Indians not too far away, and he softly called out, "Dani, come here and see if these are your people."

She came and, shading her eyes, squinted at the file of Indians and then pulled Jack back from the crest. "They are

Seri," she said. "Not Yaqui. Even if they not take me, they kill you!"

Jack carefully lifted his head and scanned the surroundings once more. Softly he said, "Now this should prove interesting. Here come the soldier boys, and they're going to meet those Indians head on!"

They watched as the soldiers, riding hard, began firing at the Indians, who split up and rode in several directions. Some of them came to the broken rocks where Jack and Dani were and took shelter behind some rocks at the lower level, from where they opened fire and shot arrows at the soldiers. The rest rode in a circle around the soldiers, shooting arrows and firing their rifles. Jack counted a dozen soldiers, out of which five were already hit. The soldiers drew up, and turning around, they rode back the way they had come, shooting to clear a way through the Indians. They were lucky that there were too few Indians to be able to cut them off, and they broke through and continued riding hard.

The Indians regrouped, and a heated discussion took place. It was obvious to Jack that some of them wanted to chase after the soldiers, but their leader was against it. After some time, the Indians continued on their way, and Jack and Dani relaxed. "Let's give it another ten minutes," said Jack, "and then we can be on our way. I don't think those soldiers are coming back anytime soon now!"

After the Indians had gone, Jack built a small smokeless fire and made some coffee, which they had with some jerky that Jack was carrying. They had water enough, and after they had drunk their fill, they gave the horses some to drink, and then they were on their way again. After another ten miles of hard riding, Jack called a halt in the shade of a towering mesa, and they let the horses rest after again sponging out their mouths and giving them a drink of water. Jack was tired, but they started again after a fifteen-minute rest.

Late that night, Dani called a halt and told Jack, "Other side of that ridge is my people. I will lead now."

She took the lead and Jack followed. As they topped the ridge, Dani shouted out in what Jack assumed must be the Yaqui tongue, and an answering shout was heard. They rode slowly forward and came to a large camp and were met by around a dozen Yaqui warriors. Jack drew some hostile stares, but Dani quickly explained to an Indian who was obviously the chief, and he listened silently. Then he held up his hand and spoke to the rest of the warriors, and Dani explained to Jack, "He is telling them that you saved me from the soldiers. No one will harm you now."

Jack spent the night with the Yaquis, and in the morning the chief sent an Indian with him to show him the shortest and safest way to the border. He said goodbye to Dani and then followed his guide to the border. They spent a night in the open, and the next morning Jack rode across the border and into New Mexico.

CHAPTER 7
ABILENE

JACK WAS HEADING BACK TO TEXAS WHEN THE CIVIL War broke out and he joined up with the Confederacy. After a year of fighting, he met up with Poco Pete and Jason Montana when they were transferred to his unit. They soon built a unit of sharpshooters and daring raiders and became known as Donovan's Ghost Raiders. That was because Jack trained them well to move silently at night, and they could move behind enemy lines better than any other unit. They would suddenly appear at a Union encampment, open fire, and then just as suddenly disappear. They never suffered any major losses on these night raids, but in general battle they took their losses like any other unit. Jack had become a Major and Jason Montana was his Captain, while Poco Pete made Lieutenant. After the order from the top brass came down that Major Donovan's unit was to be used only for night raids and not in general battle, their losses became negligible, and they became a tightly-knit fighting unit.

It was a long and bloody war, and at the end of it, they were exhausted and tired of fighting. The unit split up and Jack started drifting again. He intended to go back to Texas and the Double M, but on the way he signed up to take a herd through to Kansas for the eastern markets, where beef was desperately needed. The war had been over for less than a year and frontier towns were wild and rough. The drive ended in Abilene, and after Jack drew his wages, he decided to spend a few days in town. He took a room at a hotel and soaked in what was, for him, relaxed comfort. After all, it had been a long time since he had been able to have a proper bath daily and to shave and wear clean clothes, and for a time he reveled in it. But in three days the novelty wore off, and he missed the open range and the clean air.

He was standing at the bar in the Last Chance Saloon and nursing a drink when a trio of hard-looking men came in. They were still wearing Union army issue pants and all three wore low-slung tied-down guns. They stood at the bar and when their drinks were served, one of them said, "Here's to the Union! Death to the cowardly Confederates!" Many men in that saloon had fought for the Union and many had fought for the Confederacy, but all looked disgusted at what the trio was saying. Feelings on both sides were still raw and no one wanted to open festering wounds. Too many had died on both sides during the war and sensible people realized what a waste it had been.

Someone had slipped out and informed the town Marshal, and he now came in. Walking up to the trio, he said, "Friends, the war is over, so let's not start it up again. We're all Americans and we've all lost a lot in the war. But it's over, and here in Kansas, we intend that it stay that way. So have your drinks and do whatever you've come to town for, but lay off the war talk." He was turning to walk away when all three drew their guns and one of them said, "Turn around real slow, Marshal, there's a gun aimed right at your head!" The Marshal turned around real slow and found himself staring into the barrel of a pistol. The other two men were covering both sides of the room. The man facing the Marshal said, "Now Mister Marshal, did you fight for the Union or for the Rebs?" The Marshal was about to answer when a quiet voice said, "I fought for the Confederacy." Everyone looked to see who had spoken and the Marshal saw a six-foot two-inch tall, well-built man, dressed in range clothes, standing three feet away from the trio at the bar. He was leaning his left hand negligently against the bar, while his right hand was resting on his thigh close to his tied-down six-gun.

The trio stared at him and the one holding a gun on the Marshal said, "What did you say?"

"I fought for the Confederacy," Jack said again. "In fact, half the country did, while the other half fought for the Union. It was a wasteful war, and a bloody war, and too many people died because of it. But it's over, and we all have to get on and build our lives again." The man sneered, "We know what to do with rebel scum, don't we, boys?" He told one of the men, "Keep him covered until the Marshal here drops his gun belt and then we'll have us some fun." Jack said mildly, "I said a lot of people died because of the war, and that's a fact. Now I'm gonna tell you another fact. Unless you drop your guns right now, three more people are going to die today." The man stared and then yelled, "Get him!" All three turned to fire at Jack, but Jack was watching the man who was already facing him, and as he lifted his pistol, Jack drew. The Marshal saw only a blur of movement and then the rolling thunder of three shots that sounded as one, but he clearly saw all three men fall to the floor, dead before they hit it.

He looked at Jack, who was swiftly replacing the spent cartridges in his gun, and said, "That was fast, Mister! I ain't never seen anything faster." He added, "Figure I should thank you, they had me dead to rights and no way would I have dropped my gun belt." Jack shrugged and told him, "That's what I figured, which is why I drew cards in the game." The Marshal stuck out his hand, "The name's Blake, Blake Evans, and it's a good thing for me that you drew cards in the game." Jack shook his hand and said, "Jack Donovan, and you're welcome, although something tells me that you would have made out on your own. Sure, you would have taken their bullets, but you would have come up shooting." The Marshal was curious, "What made you think that?" Jack said softly, "There was a Union captain in an encampment that we raided. We had you dead to rights but you came up shooting all the same." The Marshal's eyes widened and he exclaimed, "That was you!? Why then you're..." Before he could say anything further, Jack said, "I'm just Jack Donovan now." The Marshal nodded and then told him, "If you would accompany me to my office, there's something I'd like to run by you."

They were seated in the Marshal's office and Blake was talking. "Since the war ended and the cattle drives began, this town has exploded," he said. "Most of the cattle drives are from Texas coming over the Chisholm Trail. The trail drive crews are tired and irritable when they reach here, because as you know, that's one tough drive." He pondered for a bit and then continued, "In general, the cowboys just want to unwind and release some steam, and that's okay because the trail bosses keep them in line and they don't generally overstep that line. But since the war ended, there are a lot of ex-soldiers from both sides who are drifting and trying to find a place to call home." Jack smiled and told him, "I'm one of them. Although I must say that I've got a place to go to, if it's still there. In fact, I'm on my way there and I just joined this cattle drive because I needed the money, and also because the trail boss is a friend and he asked me as a favor to join up. I'll be on my way by tomorrow." Blake said, "I wasn't talking about men like you, although we do get quite a few who are on their way home. They're not the problem. There are others, like the ones you just put down, who are wild and are just looking for trouble. And since this has become a boom town, there are also the thieves, the conmen, the cardsharps, and gunslingers who are attracted to all boom towns. Keeping the law in these circumstances is a tough job."

He paused for a bit, but as Jack didn't respond, he continued, "My deputy is laying in bed, wounded in a shootout, and no one wants the job right now, so I'm handling everything on my lonesome." He again paused, but again Jack didn't respond, so he sighed and said, "I'll get to the point. I want you to be my deputy." Jack started to speak but Blake raised his hand and said, "Hear me out! I know you're headed somewhere, but all I'm asking for is two weeks of your time. I've sent word for two good men whom I know, and they will be here in two weeks. By that time, my deputy will also be on his feet and we can handle things. Just two weeks, Jack?" Jack said, "I've never been a lawman, so how do you know if I can handle the job?" Blake smiled and leaned back in his chair, "I saw the way you handled yourself just now in the saloon. Besides, after that attack on my encampment, I found out a lot about Major Donovan and I was impressed." He waited a moment and then continued, "Can you handle this job? That's the least of my worries. I know you can!" Jack hesitated and then shrugged, saying, "Just two weeks!"

Blake jumped up, and opening a drawer, he withdrew a deputy's shield and pinned it on Jack. "Before you change your mind, you're sworn in!" Jack smiled and said, "You may not like my way of handling things, so I'll tell you right now. At any time, if you want me to quit, you just have to ask!" Blake shook his head and declared, "That ain't going to happen, Jack!" Then he gave Jack a thoughtful look and said, "There's one thing though, that I hope you'll clear up for me. It's been on my mind for the last three years! That night at the encampment, you had me dead to rights, but yet you missed your shot." Jack said bluntly, "It happens; could happen to anyone." But Blake shook his head and told him, "Not to you! I told you I found out a lot about Major Donovan and one of the things was that the Major doesn't waste his bullets because he never misses. It's been eating at me all these years, and I just gotta know why! You called off the attack and the Ghosts disappeared that night."

Jack looked uncomfortable, but then said, "My men also asked me the same thing and this is what I told them. We had you all dead to rights, and most of your men threw down their rifles, but you came up shooting! That was a brave thing to do, and in that instant I found I just could not kill such a brave man, war or no war. So I called off the attack." Now it was Blake who looked uncomfortable and he said, "Pretty foolhardy thing to do if you ask me." Jack smiled and retorted, "Yeah! It was that too!"

Blake changed the subject and asked Jack, "So how do you want to handle this situation?" Jack said, "By evening I'll have notices at all points of entry and in all saloons and stores. No firearms within town limits." Blake stared at him, "You're serious!" Jack said, "I sure am!" Blake went and sat down behind his desk. "Jack," he said. "Handling the drifters is one thing and maybe we can enforce the rule there, but the trail drive crews? They won't agree!" Jack said mildly, "I'll talk to them." Blake was giving him a very thoughtful look and now he said, "I just remembered, there was another rumor I heard about Major Donovan. The rumor was that he was from Texas and he had another name. Lightning Hands!" Jack raised his eyes and looked upwards and said, "I could kill you, Nate Downey!" Blake was curious and asked him, "Who's that?" Jack shook his head and then explained about the reformed bandit. "I'm sure he spread that rumor because that's what he called me there at the time." Blake gave him a thoughtful look and said, "I told you I found out a lot about the Major. Lightning Hands didn't start at that time, it started much earlier. I heard the stories about the rustlers, the shootout in the First Chance saloon, and Laredo Smith. Then there was the story of San Miguel and the five gunmen looking for revenge. Funny thing was that nobody actually knew you or who you were!" He stared at Jack and said, "I would say that Donovan's Ghosts actually started with Donovan a long time back. There were all these stories about you, but you were a ghost! Even descriptions of you varied so much that I think the only description that stuck was Lightning Hands." Jack said, "Okay, so you know all about me, but what's that got to do with the here and now?" Blake shrugged and told him, "Well, I guess those trail bosses will listen to you. So let's get this done."

They got the notices up at all entry points, and Jack rode out to meet the trail bosses of the two herds that had arrived. He explained the situation to them and laid out the new rules of no firearms in town. Brad Stewart, one of the bosses, said, "How do we know that our men will be safe in town? What if you can't uphold this law of yours and the gunslingers and army drifters pick a fight with my crew?" Len Jackson was the other trail boss, and he had been staring at Jack with a puzzled look on his face. Now his face cleared and he said, "Brad, I fought for the South, and during the war, one time a man was pointed out to me. They said he was Major Donovan, the leader of Donovan's Ghost Raiders." Turning to Jack, he said, "I knew your face was familiar, Major, and it just now come to me where I had seen you. I've heard a lot about you since then, and if you're laying down the law, then my crew will obey." Brad was still doubtful and said, "I've also heard of you, Major, and meaning no disrespect, I have to say that leading army raids is one thing, but what happens when the Tucson Kid and Sideways Joe come to town? I heard they were coming and they hate us Texans. Both are deadly, vicious, and mean, but are said to be among the fastest guns in the west." It was Len Jackson who answered him. "One thing I forgot to mention, Brad," he said. "At that time, I also heard a rumor that Major Donovan was also known as Lightning Hands before the war." Brad gave Jack a startled look and said, "That's the kid who destroyed Laredo Smith and took out five cattle rustlers on his lonesome!" He shook Jack's hand and declared, "As long as you're from Texas, I got no problem with the new law and my crew will abide by it. In fact, if you need help in dealing with any trouble, just holler and we'll all come a-running!"

Jack returned to town and told Blake that the cowboys would obey the new gun law. "Now let's go and enforce it in the saloons," he said. They went first to the Last Chance Saloon and while Blake stayed by the door holding a shotgun, Jack walked up to the bar and, going around it, he tacked a notice to the wall where everyone could see it. Coming out from behind the bar, he put his back to the counter and faced the room. "Gentlemen," he said. "From now on, the rule is no guns in town. So if you gents would hand over your guns, I would be much obliged. You can collect them from the Marshal's office when you leave town." They all stared at him without speaking and then one of the gamblers slowly stood up and faced Jack. With his hand hovering over his gun, he said, "No one is going to take my…" He did not complete his sentence but froze and slowly raised his hands as a gun seemed to appear in Jack's hand by magic. Jack said softly, "I don't want you to raise your hands, Mister; I want you to hand over your guns. Now, you can't do that with your hands raised, can you?" Blake had brought along a town loafer called Restless, who now held a large burlap sack. Jack gestured to him and he went and stood by the bar. Jack told the gambler, "You can do the honors by being the first, and the rest of you gentlemen can follow one by one." Everyone started to rise from their chairs and Jack said, "One by one, gentlemen. I'm allergic to being crowded!"

The gambler came forward and handed over his gun and Restless tied a tag to it, and the gambler wrote his name on the tag. He turned to leave and Jack said mildly, "I said guns, so that would include the one under your left armpit and maybe your sleeve gun if you have one." The gambler sighed and surrendered the guns and told Jack, "You don't miss much, do you!" Jack shrugged and told the room, "If anyone holds out on a gun and I find out about it, then you'll spend a month in jail, so no holdouts, please!" One by one everyone came and deposited their guns, which included rifles, and Blake told another regular bar hanger-on to help Restless carry the load. They went saloon by saloon, but the word had spread and nobody voiced any objections. Blake explained to Jack, "That gambler is Nick Buchanan and he's known as a deadly fast draw, so people will now think twice about bracing you."

They were seated in Blake's office, and Jack told him what Brad Stewart had said about the Tucson Kid and Sideways Joe. "That's bad news," said Blake gravely. "The Tucson Kid is hardly a kid; he's around 30 and he's credited with nine kills in straight shootouts. It's been said that he will also shoot a man in the back, but no one says it to his face. Bushwhacker or not, he is known to be deadly fast and accurate in his shooting. Sideways Joe got his name because of his habit of half-turning sideways before a shootout. Some say that he believes that it offers a smaller target for his opponent to shoot at. The word is that he's as fast if not faster than the Tucson Kid, but as they are sidekicks, I guess we'll never find out. They hunt together and yes, they hate Texans." Jack was curious and asked him, "Why Texans in particular?" Blake shrugged and explained, "The story is that when they were just starting out on their chosen career of being hired guns, they tried to tree a Texas town in a drunken fit and the townspeople caught them and whipped them before tying them to their horses and sending them on their way." Jack smiled and said, "Dime novels always write about cowboys treeing a town, not realizing that it just ain't practical. The saloon barkeep could be a former soldier, the saloon swamper could be a retired hunter, and anyway most of the people in any frontier town are armed and know how to use those arms. You just don't tree a frontier town!" Blake agreed and said, "This was many years ago and I guess they had it to learn, but that's the reason why they hate Texans."

Three days passed by peaceably and then a cowboy came

racing into town and went directly to the Marshal's office. Both Blake and Jack were there and the cowboy said, "Major, the boss said to tell you that those two yahoos, the Kid and Joe, have been spotted on their way to town. He said to tell you that they should be here in an hour and that they are coming from the south." Jack thanked him, and the cowboy left and went to a saloon. Jack told Blake, "That means they will be coming in from the other side of town. I think I'll go and welcome them to town." He got up and so did Blake, but Jack said, "No, you stay here and hold down the fort. I'll take care of this." He mounted his horse and rode out of town for about a mile to a small wooded area and tied his horse to a tree and waited by the side of the trail with his rifle in his hands.

After about half an hour, he spotted some dust in the distance and he got up and stood behind a tree and waited. Two men came riding along slowly and as they drew level with the tree, Jack aimed his rifle at them and shouted, "Hold it right there or this Henry will blow you apart!" The two men reined in their horses and placed their hands on the pommel. "Get off your horses easy like and take three steps forward," Jack told them. "And please don't try anything foolish like dismounting on the far side of the horse and drawing your guns, because I'll shoot you out of the saddle before you do." The men cursed, because that was exactly what they were going to do. Slowly, the two dismounted and walked forward, keeping their eyes on the rifle barrel because they couldn't see Jack clearly behind the tree. As Jack stepped out from behind the tree, they saw the badge on his vest and one of them said, "We've done nothing, Marshal, so why the stick-up?" Jack placed his rifle against the tree and walked forward and faced them. "Which of you is the Tucson Kid?" he asked. The man who had just spoken raised his hand, and Jack told the other man, "So that makes you Sideways Joe, I reckon." Joe nodded and asked, "What's this about, Marshal? As the Kid here said, we ain't done nothing."

Jack told them, "We have a new rule in town, no guns allowed. You can collect them when you leave. Seeing as you two are such famous gentlemen, I figured to give you the honor of telling you before you reached town." They looked at the discarded rifle and the Kid said slowly, "You put down your rifle!" Jack replied casually, "Sure, and you men can just shed your guns as well." Sideways Joe began to slowly move away from the Kid and then he started to half-turn sideways while the Kid went into the gunfighter's crouch. Before Joe could complete his sideways move, he and the Kid froze because they were staring at the six-gun in Jack's right hand. They were used to the waiting and the tenseness before guns were drawn and they hardly saw Jack palm his gun, but there it was, and they just didn't know what to do. "You can drop your gun belts now," Jack told them. "Or I can take it off after shooting you. You make your choice but make it fast!" The Tucson Kid was trembling with rage after the surprise had worn off, and he now snarled, "You want to holster that pistol and try it again…" Once more both of them froze, because before the Kid could complete what he was saying, Jack had dropped his gun in his holster and had immediately palmed it again. Sideways Joe's hand was resting on his gun butt, and he slowly moved it away. The Kid's rage melted away like snow before a fierce sun and a cold chill crept up his spine. Neither he nor Joe had really seen Jack's hand move and the speed of that move held them still. They knew they were facing death if one of them made a wrong move, and so they froze in place. "Well, gentlemen," said Jack. "Make up your minds because I'm not a patient man."

The Kid said, "If it's all the same to you, Marshal, we'll just ride back the way we came." Joe added, "Nothing particular we want to see in this town anyways, so I reckon we'll just keep riding." Jack nodded agreeably and said, "Sure thing boys, your choice." They were turning to leave when Jack added, "But you'll still leave your guns here. I don't aim to be shot in the back!" For a moment there, Jack thought the Kid was going to draw, and he was ready to shoot, but the Kid didn't want to die on a dusty trail and so he slowly unbuckled his gun belt and let it drop. Joe did the same and Jack said, "Your rifles too, and if I search your saddlebags and find another gun or if I find one on you, then I'm going to shoot you. Were I you, I'd believe me, but you do what you want." Slowly and carefully, they placed their rifles on the ground and then pulled out a spare pistol each from their saddlebags and dropped them to the ground. "Okay, you boys mount up now and you ride," said Jack. "And the next time you see me anywhere, you walk away fast because I'll be shooting and not talking!"

They mounted their horses and without a backward glance, they rode away at a fast trot. Jack collected their guns and rode back to town. When Blake asked him what had happened, all Jack said was, "They figured this town to be unhealthy, and so they left for a healthier place." Blake was curious and asked, "Without their guns?" Jack just shrugged and said, "They didn't want to carry all that weight, figured it would just slow them down." The word soon spread that the Tucson Kid and Sideways Joe were disarmed and sent on their way by Jack, and after that no one challenged the new rule in town. After Blake's new deputies arrived, Jack handed over his badge and left town.

CHAPTER 8
THE WAY BACK

HE RODE THROUGH THE BORDER OF KANSAS, ALMOST following the Chisholm Trail, and entered Oklahoma. This was Indian Territory, and most of the tribes were peaceful, with many of them joining the Confederacy to fight during the Civil War. But Jack knew that Comanche and Kiowa Indians carried out raids in the Territory, and he rode warily, using all the cover he could find. He never silhouetted himself against the skyline and only built a fire if he could make a smokeless one. Twice he saw files of Indians riding by while he was in cover, and each time he waited for a long while before riding on. He started out before daybreak every day and only stopped for the night when he found a reasonably safe place to sleep.

One morning as he was starting out, he heard gunshots and the bellowing of cattle. Riding hard towards the sound, he crested a rise and saw a cattle drive being attacked by Indians. It was the Indian way to attack just before dawn, when most people would be less alert, although the Indian would rarely attack at night, as they believed that if they were killed in battle at night then their soul would wander in darkness forever. He saw some cowboys trying their best to keep the herd from stampeding, while others were shooting at the Indians who were riding in a circle around the camp. It was open land where the drive had stopped for the night, and Jack figured that the trail boss was a canny man. In such an open area, the Indians could not lay siege or hide behind rocks; the only way that they could attack was by a frontal assault. Jack figured that there were around twenty-five Indians attacking the camp, which was quite a large raiding party.

Unsheathing his rifle, he rode down the slope at a walk and began picking his targets, firing rapidly. Before the Indians could realize that there was another guest at the party, Jack had shot four of them. Ten of the Indians swung around and rode towards Jack, firing as they came. Jack coolly dismounted, and keeping his horse in front of him, continued firing over the saddle. His horse was well-trained in battle and stood still, except for a nervous snort and a twitch of the tail from time to time. Jack shot another five Indians before the rest gave up and swerved away. Whether the Indians he shot were dead or wounded, there was no way to be sure, because those that fell off their horses were swept up by the others on the run, while others who were hit clung tightly to their horses and raced away.

As soon as the Indians swung away, Jack was immediately in the saddle and riding forward again, looking for targets. Caught between the cowboys on one side and Jack on the other, the Indians called it quits and rode away, taking their wounded and dead with them. Jack had reached the camp by then and saw a group of cowboys come charging out of the camp on horses in pursuit of the running Indians.

"Hold it!" he yelled. "Hold up, fellas! Don't ride after them!"

A man came running out of the camp and told the cowboys to stop. He walked up to Jack and held out his hand.

"Wes Blaine," he told Jack. "I'm mighty thankful to you for taking cards in the game. You saved the herd, as they were getting ready to stampede at any moment."

Jack shook his hand and said, "Jack Donovan, heading back to Texas. Heard the shots and figured it was a stampede or an Indian attack."

One of the cowboys who had been stopped from chasing the Indians asked Jack, "Why tell us to stop? We had them on the run, and we could have finished the job instead of letting them get away."

Jack said, "Those were Comanche, and I spotted two large groups a few days ago. This here is a well-planned camp in the open, and it gave you the advantage. If you were to chase them now, they would keep running until they came to a place that would shift the advantage to them. Then they would stop and fight, and if they are meeting up with another group, you wouldn't stand a chance."

Wes Blaine said, "He's right, Tom, never go chasing after Indians, because they will run only until they can seize the advantage." Turning to Jack, he said, "Come into the camp and have some coffee and breakfast. We're going to have to quiet down the herd before we can move on, or for sure they'll stampede at even a shadow!"

As they walked into the camp, he asked Jack, "Think they'll be back?"

Jack shrugged and told him, "You never know with the Comanche. They've taken losses here, and they'll think that their medicine has turned bad, and normally they won't be back. But as I said, I've seen other groups, and if they meet up, then they might be back. This is a large herd, and it means a plentiful supply of meat for them. You're going to have to ride real careful over the next two or three days."

Hunkered down by the fire, drinking coffee, Blaine asked Jack, "So you're from Texas?"

Jack hesitated and then said, "Not exactly. You see, I drifted there twelve years ago and took on with the Double M at Cedar Creek. I left after two years, and then the war came, and it's taken me this long to get back again." After a moment, he added, "The Double M is the closest thing to family for me, and I guess I've been missing them."

Blaine looked worried, and he said seriously, "The word is that the Double M is in trouble, something to do with carpetbaggers trying to take over the ranch." He gave Jack a thoughtful look and said, "Funny thing is, people say that there was a kid named Jack at the Double M a while back, and they say that if he was there now, he would run those carpetbaggers right out of the country."

Jack stood up, saying, "I'm obliged to you, but I got to ride and ride fast."

Blaine also stood up and asked him, "You're the kid that they talk about, ain't you?"

Jack just nodded his head, and Blaine said, "Well, you can't ride fast on just one horse, so as a thank you for saving my herd, I'm giving you two good horses."

When Jack started to protest, Blaine held up his hand and said, "You ain't gonna insult me by refusing my gift, now are you? Besides, with the Double M in trouble, you're going to have to ride hard and fast."

Jack thanked him, and Blaine yelled out to a cowboy who then brought two fine-looking horses and handed them over to Jack. Before leaving, he told Blaine, "Do me a favor and just pass the word along the trails that the Double M is in trouble, and Jack needs Jason Montana, like yesterday!"

He rode hard and he rode fast, switching horses every now and then to conserve their energy, wondering all the time if the McCullough family was still holding out. Wherever he stopped, he passed along the same message that he needed Jason Montana. One day, he was riding one of Blaine's horses and had just stopped to switch the saddle to another horse, when in the distance he saw a dust cloud. Quickly cinching the saddle and transferring his blanket roll and saddlebags, he mounted up and rode away. But the delay brought the dust cloud nearer, and turning in the saddle, he saw that it was an Indian war party. He urged the horses on, and the Indians began shooting even before they were in range. Riding hard, he felt a tug on the lead rope, and looking back he saw that one of the horses had been hit and was starting to flounder. He unsheathed his knife and sliced the lead rope that tethered the horse to his saddle, and bending low over his horse, he coaxed it on to greater speed. Looking back, he saw that the Indians were now well within rifle range, so he took his rifle and half turning in his saddle, he began firing rapidly at them. He saw one Indian fall from his horse, and the rest immediately slowed their run, but Jack urged his horse on and soon left the Indians far behind. He slowed his horse to a canter and then a walk, and finally stopped when he reached a small wood. He rubbed down the horses and let them graze and rest while he stood guard watching his back trail. It took another three days before he finally rode into Cedar Creek.

CHAPTER 9
THE DOUBLE M

"So Maria died," said Jack sadly. "How I wish I could have been there!" He sighed, then shook himself and said, "But tell me about the present trouble that you folks are having. And why didn't you send word along the trails? I would have been here sooner."

Bruce just shrugged and told him, "The War happened, I guess. We heard that you had joined up on the side of the Confederacy but heard nothing after that. What happened here was that the carpetbaggers came to town and rode roughshod over everyone, but Dad held out and so did the Rafter K, which is a ranch adjoining ours. The ranch started a few years after you left and they're good folks. They're from Tennessee and a more hardworking, close-knit family would be hard to find, I reckon. Also, there's no give to them and they ride straight and proud. We had twelve hands but we're down to ten now, and the Rafter K has five hands. But then they have old man Bailey with his old Sharps rifle, and he never misses. He's a widower with five children, four boys and one girl, and they can all shoot and fight. Believe me, there's no give to any of them, so together we've managed to hold out. But now Dan White, he's the trouble-making carpetbagger, has brought in some serious guns for hire, and things are getting tough."

Jack doused the fire with water from the kettle, then threw some sand on it and stamped around a bit to make sure that there were no embers left. "Let's ride," he told Bruce. "You can catch me up with everything when we hit the ranch." They rode hard and fast as Jack was eager to see the old ranch that he had missed so much over the intervening years.

They rode into the front yard, swung down from their saddles and hitched their horses to the hitching rail. Jack looked around and felt a pang of nostalgia, as nothing much had changed in the ten years that he had been gone. He almost expected to see Maria come to the front door with that welcoming smile of hers. They walked up to the porch, and the front door swung open. Jack stopped in his tracks as though he had run into a brick wall. For a moment, he thought that he was looking at Maria, but soon realized that the young lady who stood in the doorway was Beth. But a grown-up Beth, and a very beautiful Beth, he thought, who also had her mother's golden hair just like Bruce. Beth stood there for a moment, staring at him, and then suddenly screamed and ran straight to him, hugging him tight.

"Jack, Jack," she cried. "I knew that you would come back, I just knew it!" She pulled back and, holding him by the waist, she searched his face and what she saw there made her feel sad.

"You're different, Jack," she said. "It's not just that you're a full-grown man now, but it's your eyes. They look tired and kind of bleak."

Jack shrugged and smiled, saying, "You're different too, Beth. All growed up and so beautiful and graceful; and here I was still picturing the little girl who would never leave me alone!"

A sudden shyness came over Beth and she flushed, pulling away from him. "Come on in and I'll make some coffee," she said. "Dad will be in soon from the range."

They were sitting around the dining table drinking coffee, and Jack asked Bruce, "Any of the old crowd still around?"

Bruce looked sad as he said, "Our old cook Thomas is still here and the three old timers I told you about. Will Dorsey came back from the war and came straight here to join up. He's out on the range with Dad, I reckon." He hesitated and then said, "Jack, Billy and Clyde also came back. They went into town last week and two of Dan White's hired guns forced a fight and shot them dead. I'm sorry, Jack."

Jack sighed and asked him, "So that's why you were in town today pretending to be drunk? Looking to settle scores?"

Beth said, "He wanted to go to town immediately after and call them out, but Dad wouldn't have it. Today, with Dad away, he sneaked out and went to town, and I've been so worried. I've seen those hired guns and they're hard-looking men with reputations for killing behind them."

Bruce shrugged and then said, "But how did you know about our troubles, Jack? Those two in the bar were part of Dan White's crew. They claim to be cowhands but no one has ever seen them work the range."

Jack told him, "I was on my way here and starting out one morning when I came upon Indians attacking a cattle drive, so I rode up and took a hand in the game with my Henry rifle. That broke the attack and the Indians vanished. The trail boss insisted that I stay and break bread with them. Sitting at the campfire, I said that I was on my way back to the Double M as I had left ten years ago and it had taken me this long to get back again. The trail boss, Blaine, mentioned that the Double M was in trouble with carpetbaggers trying to take over the ranch. He gave me two horses for helping to fight the Indians, so I could ride hard and fast to get here by switching horses without stopping to rest."

Bruce said, "So that's why you didn't want me to let on that I knew you when you walked into the bar."

Jack told him, "I wanted to look the situation over first, and when I saw those two gunslingers give the nod to the man bracing you, I knew it was a trap set for you, so I took a hand in the game."

Just then there was the sound of pounding hooves and a moment later Ryan and Will Dorsey charged into the room. Both of them stared at Jack for a moment and then ran to him and began pounding his back. Finally they let up and Ryan looked long and hard at Jack.

"The years haven't been good to you, Jack," he said softly. "It was a bad war, wasn't it!"

Jack shrugged and said, "Bad enough, but I made it through; too many didn't."

Beth told him, "Dad joined up and was in it for two years, and then was invalided out. He still doesn't have full use of his right hand."

They all sat down and Ryan told Jack about the current situation. Dan White was a carpetbagger who came to town and rode roughshod over everyone. He had come to the ranch and told Ryan to sell out to him.

"He didn't ask," Ryan said. "He ordered me to sell him the ranch, and the price he named was laughable, so I laughed."

Beth chimed in, "He had three men with him and things might have turned bad, but just then Old man Bailey and two of his sons rode up. They had come to ask Dad for some ranching advice, and when he saw what was happening he rode up to Dan White and in a clear voice told him to get off the ranch. He was holding his Sharps across his saddle and his sons were at the back of the men with their rifles in their hands, so Dan White got off the ranch."

Ryan told Jack, "They're from the hills of Tennessee, and they've travelled far before finally settling here to build a new life."

Jack smiled and said, "I've met a few of those mountain men.

Taciturn, and no scare to them, and they're the best sharpshooters I've ever seen. They're also mighty clannish and they stand by each other and their friends. Good men to have at your side in times of trouble."

"Dan White is on the old Porter ranch," Ryan continued. "Old man Porter's sons died in the war, and Dan White claims he bought the property, but no one believes him because old man Porter disappeared. Dan White claims that Porter was broken by the loss of his sons and so he sold him the property and lit out of town. He now has his eyes on the Double M and the Rafter K. By the way, the K stands for Bailey's wife Kate, who didn't make it to Texas. She was killed during an Indian attack the same as Maria." He looked sad and was quiet for a moment and then added, "I really miss her." He looked at Jack and said, "She'd be happy knowing that you're back where you belong. No more drifting, Jack!"

Jack nodded and then said, "Jason Montana was with me in a few battles during the war and I've sent him word along the line that the Double M is in trouble. If he can, he will be here soon, and he's a good man to have at your side."

Beth stood up and told him, "You look exhausted, Jack. I'll make up your old room and you can get some sleep after you've eaten."

Jack smiled and told her, "That sure sounds good. I've been riding hard for the past two weeks to get here."

Jack awoke before the break of dawn as was his habit. Tired as he had been, he had dropped into a deep sleep as soon as his head had hit the pillow. Now he felt rested and ready to face whatever fate had in store for him. He frowned as he thought about Billy and Clyde and the way that they had been gunned down. They weren't gunslingers, they were just very good ranch hands, and no one was better than the two brothers when it came to roping and branding a wild steer or breaking in a bucking bronco. They were born to the saddle, and the lariat was an extension of their hands. They must have known that the men who braced them were hired gunmen and that no one would have thought less of them if they had refused to draw. But they had always lived by their code of honor, and now they had died by it. Jack's face turned bleak and he whispered, "I'll even the score for you, Billy."

He washed up, dressed in clean clothes from his carpetbag, and then went searching for breakfast. Beth was in the dining room laying out his breakfast when he came in. She looked up, smiled, and said, "I heard you get up and I figured you would want breakfast in a hurry after that dead sleep. You do look rested now." Jack was hungry, so he sat down and demolished the pile of freshly baked bread with six eggs and fried ham and bacon. Finally he sighed and sat back contentedly, only to find Beth looking at him with a bemused expression.

"You must have been starving," she said with a smile. "You didn't once look up while you were eating."

Jack grimaced and said, "I apologize for my lack of manners. Guess I've been too long on the trail. Come to think of it, the last time I ate in a house with a family was right here, ten years ago!"

Beth turned serious and asked him, "You'll stay here now, won't you, Jack? You won't leave us again?"

Jack looked at her serious face and said, "I'll stay, Beth." Then he got up, saying, "But right now there are some things that I have to do. Where's Will and your Dad?"

"They're here," said Beth. "They get up very early now as there's lots to do on the range, but they were waiting for you to get up. Dad said not to disturb you as you seemed pretty exhausted last night."

They went out to the porch and found Ryan sitting there, and from the bunkhouse Will Dorsey and Bruce came running up. The first question Jack asked was, "Do you know who the hombres were who gunned down Billy and Clyde?"

Will Dorsey told him, "Leon Mendoza and Jake Rawlings. From what I've heard, Leon is around 28 years old and real fast with a gun. He is reputed to have 15 killings to his name, some of them south of the border. He's mean and cruel, Jack! From what folks say, he was the one who taunted Billy when Clyde at first refused to draw. Jake Rawlings is just a hired killer who they say would as soon shoot you in the back as face you."

Ryan said, "What are you planning on doing, Jack? I've sent word for the Bailey family to come over so that we can sort of have a council of war."

Jack said mildly, "Why, I just thought I'd take me a ride into town just to see how things look after ten years. There must be a lot of changes now."

Just then, old man Bailey and two of his sons rode into the yard. They hitched their horses and came up the steps to the porch, and Ryan introduced them, "Jack, this here is Nolan Bailey and his sons Mike and Luke."

After the introduction, Ryan said, "Well, let's go sit inside and talk. We have to have a plan to deal with Dan White, because if we just wait around, he will slowly but surely whittle us down. They do say that some of the hired guns he has are bushwhackers too."

Jack said casually, "You folks go ahead and plan and I'll go along with what you decide. Right now, I just want to see the old town; must be getting nostalgic as I grow older."

He stepped off the porch and went to saddle his horse. Mike and Luke looked at each other and then Mike asked Bruce, "That the man who took out five rustlers and beat Laredo Smith to a pulp?"

Bruce nodded and the two brothers stood up. "Well, Paw," Mike told their father. "Guess we better get to town and see if they have that calico cloth that Betsy wants."

Old man Bailey stared at his sons and then glanced at Jack

77

saddling his horse. "Don't try no fancy stuff, boy," he growled. "Just keep your rifles handy."

Luke shrugged and said mildly, "Oh, we ain't gonna be doing nothing, Paw! I just want to see Leon Mendoza's face when he realizes he's up against ole 'Lightning Hands' there."

At Bruce's puzzled expression, Mike laughed, "You didn't know? We heard about that man yonder a long time ago. They were calling him Lightning Hands then. Before the war, he accounted for five glory-hunting gunslingers who went searching for him. Word is that those gunslingers were real fast and real hard men, but after ole Lightning Hands planted them in Boot Hill, the desire to brace him sort of tapered off, I reckon, and no one else went searching for him. When we were in Gila City during the gold rush, we heard that he had broken up a gang of bandits who were killing miners and stealing their gold."

Jack was halfway to town when he heard the horses behind him, and turning in the saddle he saw the two brothers. So he pulled up and waited until they reached him.

"Did Ryan send you?" he asked them.

"Whatever are you talking about!" exclaimed Mike innocently. "Our sister Betsy has been hounding us for some calico cloth and we're going to town to see if they have any."

Jack sighed, then laughed and told them, "Okay, let's ride. Just do me a favor and stay out of it, okay?"

Luke asked him innocently, "Yes, sir! But if anyone tries to shoot you in the back?"

Jack smiled and told him, "Then I'd be obliged if you'd take a hand."

They continued riding to town and Jack found himself instinctively liking the two brothers as they talked on the way. Mike was the eldest brother at 28, a year older than Jack. Luke was the youngest boy at 20, and there was Brian who was 25, and Mark who was 23. Betsy was the youngest at 18.

CHAPTER 10
LEON MENDOZA

They rode into town, three tall young men, broad-shouldered and slim-waisted, with their pistols in their holsters and their rifles butt forward in their sheaths. They were young men in age but old in experience, old beyond their years, for that was the land and the time they lived in. Jack knew that he could rely on the Baileys, for they came from a feuding family, and they cut their baby teeth on a rifle. In the Tennessee Mountains, even a ten-year-old youngster could bark a squirrel with his rifle for his supper; they learned early, or they went hungry.

They hitched their horses to the rail and walked into The First Chance Saloon with their rifles in their hands. At the batwing doors, they stopped and looked in, and Mike told Jack, "See that slim hombre at the bar, all dressed up in black? That's Leon Mendoza, and the ranny standing next to him with the gun holstered on the right and the knife sheathed on the left is Jake Rawlings. I hear tell that he fancies himself with that knife." Jack pushed the batwing doors open, and they trooped in. Jack went straight to the bar, but the brothers split up; Mike went left while Luke went right until they had their backs to the wall and could cover the entire room with their rifles. There was a smattering of townsfolk and three tough-looking men playing cards at a table, who Jack assumed were on Dan White's payroll. Jack walked up to the bar and said, "Whiskey, the good stuff." He was standing a few feet away to the left of Leon Mendoza and Jake Rawlings. When the barkeep came over to pour his drink, Jack carefully leant his rifle against the bar, and picking up the glass with his left hand, he remarked, "You're new here. What happened to ole Will Cook?" The barkeep said shortly, "He retired. This here bar's under new management now." Jack smiled and said in a slightly louder voice, "You don't say! New management, huh? Would that new management be Dan White, the carpetbagger?"

Suddenly there was pin-drop silence in the room, and Leon Mendoza turned slowly to face Jack. "You must be desperate to get to Boot Hill, stranger," he said. Jack placed his drink, untouched, on the counter and turned slowly to face him. "Oh, I ain't a stranger hereabouts. In fact, in this town, I'm as old as the hills," he said. With a knowing smirk, he added, "I'm here looking for a little weasel who goes by the name of Leon Mendoza. I hear tell that he fancies himself as a gunslinger." Leon went absolutely still, and he stared at Jack for a moment. "I'm Leon," he said softly. "But you knew that already, didn't you!" It was a statement and not a question, for Leon was puzzled and wary. He had survived for so long because he never trusted the obvious, and he did not for a moment believe that Jack was just some loudmouth cowboy trying to make a name for himself. Jack's face turned bleak, and he said softly, "I knew! I also know that you gunned down two good friends of mine, Billy and Clyde Hadden. For that, you will die today."

There was a collective soft sigh from the room because the words were not said in anger or in a threatening voice, but calmly, as though there could be no doubt in the matter at all. Leon felt a chill creep up his spine; there was something about this man...but he shrugged off the feeling. He was Leon Mendoza, and today he would kill this brash young man. He drew with flashing speed and smiled to himself. 'Now you will die from the gun of Leon Mendoza,' he was thinking to himself. 'They will add you to my tally, and they will talk about how...' The thought trailed away as he felt a blow to his chest and felt himself falling...falling...and then he was on the ground, half-leaning against the wall of the room. As his mind started to cloud over, he realized that he wasn't holding his gun in his hand, and he glanced down and saw that the gun was still in its holster. 'How can that be...' he started to think, and then everything went black, and Leon Mendoza would never kill another man.

Leon had started his draw when Jack shot him through the heart. As he fell, Jack said, "Jake Rawlings, you're next." He sheathed his pistol and stood waiting. Jake Rawlings licked his lips and stared at the fallen Mendoza and then at Jack. It had happened so fast that he hadn't even started to reach for his gun. Just then, there were two loud clicks of rifle hammers being drawn back. "Everyone just stay put, and you'll live a little longer. That goes especially for you three yahoos," Mike said, lifting his rifle slightly to point at the three hired guns who were sitting and gambling at a table. Luke added, "You all would oblige us by placing your hands on the table where we can see them." The three hired guns just stared at him sullenly, and Luke shrugged. "Or not, and I'll just put a bullet in one of you," he said and tilted his rifle barrel. All three of them slapped their hands on the table and kept them there while glaring at Luke.

"I'm waiting," Jack told Rawlings. But Rawlings looked again at Mendoza and said, "I ain't goin' to draw against you. You want to kill me, you got to do it in cold blood." Jack grimaced and said, "I hear tell that that's what you do, just wait around and bushwhack someone. Drop your gun belt!" Slowly and carefully, Rawlings unbuckled his gun belt and let it drop to the floor. Jack holstered his pistol and said, "I also hear that you fancy yourself with that toothpick you carry around. Take out your knife and let's see if you're as good as you think." Rawlings' eyes lit up, and he drew his knife. "You just made the biggest mistake in your life, Mister," he said with an evil grin. Suddenly, the grin vanished, for Jack had reached back and drawn his Bowie knife from the sheath hanging between his shoulder blades. Rawlings began to circle, but Jack started walking straight up to him and began crowding him towards the wall. Rawlings crouched a bit, and when Jack was within range, he made a slash at his gut. Fast as he was, the knife never reached Jack. In a flash of movement, Jack's left hand slapped downwards and deflected the knife while his right hand slashed across Rawlings' throat, and the Bowie knife cut to the bone. Again a sigh rose from the room as Rawlings fell dead. They were expecting to see a knife fight, but this one was over before it had even started. They just could not believe the flashing speed of Jack's hands.

Jack sheathed his knife and looked at the three toughs at the table and said, "Stand up!" Slowly the three stood up, and Jack said, "Drop your gun belts and leave. Go tell Dan White that I'm hunting him now, so he can stay here and die, or he can go back to where he came from." The three men just stared at Jack. He sighed and told them, "You can drop your gun belts or I'll put a bullet through your kneecap. The choice is yours!" They looked at each other and slowly unbuckled their gun belts and let them drop. Then they just as slowly walked towards the door without looking back or making any sudden movements. Jack picked up his rifle and headed out of the bar, and the two brothers backed out behind him. They mounted their horses and left town at a trot while keeping a wary eye all around to check for any ambush. As soon as they had left the bar, the room erupted, with everyone talking at once. The house gambler went over to Mendoza and examined him. "Straight through the heart," he announced. "And he couldn't even get his gun out." A grizzled old man said, "I seen a lot in my time, but I never seen the likes of this man! No extra talk, just straight to the point, and he goes for the kill! That there's a man to walk around of; a long way around!"

Riding side by side to the ranch, Mike looked at Jack and said, "No wonder they called you Lightning Hands! Man, I hardly saw your hands move! That was no knife fight, that was a slaughter; and Rawlings had a name for being a mean knife fighter!" Jack asked him, "You knew who I was?" Luke laughed and said, "From the get-go! Why you think we came along, Jack? We wanted to see you in action, and boy was that *action*!" Jack changed the subject and asked them, "How many men does Dan White have?" Mike thought for a bit and then said, "Well, it's like this, Jack. He has around twenty men, or I should say he *had* around twenty men. You've whittled that down by taking out Leon Mendoza and Rawlings. Besides that, you incapacitated two more when you rode into town, so I would say around fifteen or sixteen left. But here's the thing, Jack; he has Matt Duncan, who is just about 22 years old, I'd reckon, and is known as the fastest gun in the West. He's known to have killed four men in fair shootouts, and at least two of them were real professional gunmen. Then he has Nat Hardy, about 24 years of age, and who folks say is as fast as Matt Duncan; some swear that he's faster. He has around 12 killings to his name, and some say there are more that no one knows about because he doesn't boast, and he's a taciturn man who keeps to himself. But where Matt Duncan will always give you a fair fight, the same can't be said of Hardy, who folks say was born with a real mean streak. Then there is Black Wind, who claims to be 30, but no one can really say how old he is. He's a half-breed tracker and hunter of men, skilled in the use of the knife and a dead shot with his rifle. His gun is always for hire, but he won't brace his target face to face. He's given a target and he will patiently track and hunt the man down, and then kill him from ambush. Those are the real fighters and the real danger; the rest are just followers, although hard men all the same who won't back down, and some of them are genuine fast-draw experts, just not in the same class as Matt and Hardy or, for that matter, Leon." Jack asked him, "And what about Dan White, how does he stack up?" Mike shrugged and said, "No one knows, although there are whispers that Dan White is not his real moniker, and that he was a pirate and smuggler who saw a good opportunity in the Civil War and fought on the side of the Yankees as a cover for his smuggling, which made him a lot of money."

"If he made a lot of money, then why is he here?" asked Jack. "Ryan thinks that he now wants power," explained Mike. "If he takes control of all the ranches in this area, then that gives him standing in the community, and with his money to back him, he will be a contender for Governor of Texas." Jack said thoughtfully, "I think Ryan may be right. He will bring in hired killers and take the land by force and murder if necessary, and when he is in possession, he will make sure that there is no one left to talk about what he did, and he will assume a cloak of respectability. It's been tried before."

CHAPTER II
NAT HARDY

THEY RODE UP TO THE RANCH HOUSE TO FIND OLD man Bailey still sitting there with Ryan and Beth. Bailey's other two sons, Brian and Mark, and his daughter Betsy were also there. Everyone listened silently while Luke narrated what had happened in town. Then Ryan said, "The Marshal will be along soon to try and arrest you, Jack." Mike exploded, "But it was a fair fight and there were witnesses!" Jack asked Ryan, "Bob King not around?" Ryan said bitterly, "He was the first casualty. They called it a fair fight, but how fair can it be when Nat Hardy forced the fight on him! Now they have their puppet in place, Brad Cooper. He came in with Dan White and opened a general store, although he's never there and it's run by another man who came in with him. The Marshal will do whatever Dan White says." Luke snorted and said angrily, "We're not going to stand by and let the Marshal take Jack, are we?" Mike said mildly, "If you had listened, kid, instead of talking, you would have heard Ryan say that the Marshal would *try*." Just then there was a pounding of hooves, and a group of men rode into the yard. Brian and Mark had disappeared from the porch as soon as they had spotted the dust in the distance. Jack had been standing by the horses, but now he was mounted as he watched the men pull up in a cloud of dust. Old man Bailey was still sitting, but now he had his Sharps rifle resting casually on the porch railing but pointing in the direction of the riders. Mike and Luke had split up and were standing at opposite ends of the porch with their rifle barrels resting easily in the crook of their left arms.

Ryan stepped off the porch and confronted the group of men. There were around six men, including the Marshal, who was leading them. "What can I do for you, Cooper?" said Ryan. He refused to call him Marshal, because by Ryan's code, Cooper was just Dan White's lapdog and not worthy of being called Marshal. "I've come to arrest the killer who murdered two fine upstanding citizens of the town today," Cooper said pompously. "Did I hear you right?" said old man Bailey, leaning slightly forward as though to hear better, but now the Sharps was pointing straight at Cooper. He looked at Ryan, "Did he say upstanding citizens?" It was Mike who answered, "Sure sounded like it, but the dust they just raised must be causing us to hear wrong." Luke said, "Of course you heard wrong, Mike! Do you think any Marshal would call Leon Mendoza or Jake Rawlings upstanding citizens? You couldn't find two worse rattlesnakes if you searched the whole of Texas!" Cooper started to bluster, but Jack had casually moved his mount so that he was facing the six men from the side and now he said, "There were enough witnesses that it was a fair fight. I'm the man you're looking for and I say that it was a very fair fight. Do you want to call me a liar?" Cooper stared at him and turned slightly pale.

Cooper had heard something of what had happened in the bar, and he had no wish to go after a man who could take care of Mendoza and Rawlings together without raising a sweat. But Dan White had told him to arrest Jack, and he had played it safe by taking along five men with him. One of the men was Nat Hardy, a notoriously short-tempered man, who now pushed his horse to the front and dismounted, leaving the reins dangling. He took two steps forward and looking up at Jack, he said, "Get down off that horse and ask me that question again." Jack dismounted and walked forward, and when he was at a distance of not more than ten feet from Hardy, Ryan suddenly said, "You needed Nat Hardy to give you some backbone, Cooper?" It was so patently a warning for Jack that Hardy glanced at Ryan and gave him a cold smile. Jack was about to stop, but hearing the name, he continued walking a bit faster and before Hardy realized it, Jack was just a foot away and staring into his face. "I said it was a fair fight," repeated Jack. "Do you want to call me a liar?" Everyone could see that Hardy was flustered. No sane man stood just a foot away from his opponent during a shootout, as both men would surely die. A fast draw wasn't of much value at such close range, as all the slower man had to do was grab onto his opponent and then shoot. Only a head shot could ensure that that did not happen, but with the space between them being just one foot, a head shot wasn't possible.

Jack was aware of the danger, but he never intended to draw his gun. His plan was to sow a little uncertainty in the minds of the hired guns of Dan White. Until now, they were supremely confident that they would win as the odds were stacked against the ranchers, none of whom had gunslingers on their payroll. If Hardy tried to draw, then Jack had a plan, and he was confident in his ability to carry it off. Nat Hardy was a sullen-looking, pale-faced man of slight build who had never done a hard day's work in his life, as he depended on his skill with his gun and would never get into a fistfight. Now his pale face went even paler as Jack again repeated the question. He tried to slowly step back, but Jack crowded him and did not let the space between them increase. Seeing what was happening, Cooper blustered, "Now see here, I'm the Marshal, and you talk to me!" There was a loud snick of a rifle hammer, and old man Bailey said mildly, "You've said your piece, Cooper, now shut it or you'll be talking through a great big hole the size of a barn door in that belly of yours."

Nat Hardy was desperate and confused. He had never been in a situation like this before, and although he was no coward, he wasn't foolhardy enough to try a shootout in this setup. He again tried to move back, but this time Jack moved forward and suddenly slapped his face hard. Hardy stood transfixed for a moment with surprise, then with a bellow of rage he drew his gun. Rather, he tried to draw his gun, but with his gun just out of the holster, he felt his hand crushed in a strong grip and found that he couldn't raise his hand. The grip tightened and crushed his fingers against the butt of the gun, and he cried out in pain as the gun fell from his nerveless fingers. Old man Bailey was staring in awe at Jack. He had seen the flashing speed of Hardy's draw, but he never saw Jack's hand move; but there it was, crushing Hardy's fingers until he dropped his gun. There were loud snicks of rifle hammers being drawn back, and Brian and Mark came around from the two sides of the house with their rifles pointed at the group of men on horses. Cooper looked up and saw that Mike and Luke also had their rifles pointing in the same direction. Old man Bailey said, "You men carefully get down from those horses and move to the side. Don't make any move that we might find suspicious because then we'll just naturally have to shoot you." With Cooper still trying to bluster, the other men got off their mounts very carefully, and with their hands raised, they moved to one side. Cooper looked around, and seeing that he was all alone, he hastily dismounted and joined the other men.

Jack still retained his grip on Hardy's gun hand with his left hand, and he now had Hardy's left hand in his right. Hardy was struggling to get free, but Jack was big and strong, and his hands were like iron bands that held Hardy effortlessly. Suddenly, he released Hardy and then slapped him hard again, and as Hardy stumbled back, he slapped him repeatedly, right and left, and then right and left again. Hardy fell down, but Jack picked him up and held him with his left hand while continuing to slap him with his right until Hardy hung limp and moaning in his grip with blood dribbling out of his open mouth. It was brutal, and the ranch yard was shrouded in silence as everyone just stared in awe at what was happening. Every man there knew that Jack had just broken Nat Hardy in the worst possible way. This was the West, and Hardy would never be able to live down the slapping. A fight was different, and even the loser was respected for the way he fought. But this wasn't a fight, this was a man being slapped silly without being able to do anything about it. The aura of menace that hung over men like Hardy had just disappeared like a puff of smoke, and no man would ever again look in fear at Hardy; not after this story of the slapping broke.

Still holding onto the almost senseless and bleeding Hardy, Jack dragged him over and threw him at Cooper's feet. His face was remorseless, and his blue eyes were cold and bleak as he asked Cooper, "I said that the fight in town was fair. Do you want to call me a liar?" Cooper was trembling, and he opened and shut his mouth, but no words came through, and Jack repeated the question. "It was fair, it was fair," cried Cooper. "I believe you, it was fair." Jack stared at him and then said, "And was this fight fair?" Cooper nodded his head and went on nodding it as he almost cried out, "Yes, yes, this was fair, I will swear it was fair!" Jack said softly, "So what are you still doing here then? There's a smell coming off you that I just don't like." Cooper licked his lips and looked wildly all around, and then almost ran for his horse. The other men slowly followed, and one of them spat after Cooper in disgust, bent and picked up Hardy, and carried him to put him on his horse. Then the cavalcade rode out of the ranch at a fast pace, with Cooper leading the way. Jack watched them for a while and then turned around and climbed the steps to the porch. "I just figured to shake the confidence of the rest of the hired guns in Dan White's invincibility," he told Ryan. "I took no pleasure in that." Ryan held his shoulders and looked him in the eye and said, "I know that, son, because I know you." Luke was jubilant and exclaimed, "Now do you all see why they call him Lightning Hands? His left is just as fast as his right!" Old man Bailey told Jack, "Son, all I got to say is, I'd rather have you as a friend than an enemy!" Everyone laughed, and the mood lightened as the tension eased.

CHAPTER 12
BETH

LATE THAT EVENING, JACK WAS SITTING ON THE porch steps, just soaking in the stillness of the night, when Beth came and sat down by his side.

"Mother loved the calm and the peace of the night," Beth said. "Whenever she could, she would sit here on these steps and just gaze up at the stars in the sky."

Jack sighed and said, "I remember. One night I was setting out for my shift of night riding on the herd, and here she was sitting, just looking up at the sky." After a moment, he added, "I sure do miss her. She was the mother I never had."

Beth said, "I miss her too, we all do. I cried every night for a month after she was gone. She was such a warm and loving person." She was silent for a bit, then said, "It's strange, isn't it, that both our mothers died during an Indian attack. Do you remember anything at all about your parents, Jack?"

He shook his head and told her, "The old scout who took me in told me that I was just barely two years old at the time. He told me that he took me in to repay the kindness and warmth of my mother. He was what they called a half-breed, but he said that she always treated him as though he was no different from anyone else. He said that he respected her because she always treated him with respect."

A companionable silence enveloped them for a while, and then Beth stirred and said, "Everybody is talking about the speed of your hands, Jack. Old man Bailey said that he'd never seen the like in all his born days. How did you get so fast?"

Jack was silent for a moment and then said, "When I was about ten years old, my adoptive father took on a job of scouting and hunting for the railroad in an area of the Midwest where they were laying new track at the time. The cook for the railroad crew was a Chinese, and he used to look after me when my father was out hunting meat for the pot." He looked contemplative for a bit and then said with a half-smile, "I was always fast with my hands and big for my age. At the age of ten, I could draw a pistol from my waistband with considerable speed and put a bullet exactly where I intended. This Chinese cook started teaching me an art of fighting that he said was native to his country. It was bare-hands fighting, but it was nothing like the knuckle-and-skull dirty fighting that I was used to seeing. There was a kind of grace and fluidity in the way he moved. He told me that to become a master of that art would take many years of training. So instead, he concentrated on teaching me some moves that he said would help me take down a much bigger man without any trouble. He also taught me a kind of concentration, which I have practiced ever since."

Beth was puzzled and asked him, "What kind of concentration?"

Jack shifted a bit and then said hesitantly, "It's difficult to describe. I breathe in a certain way and kind of concentrate my energy in the center of my body; and then when I move, there is an explosiveness to the move." He shrugged uncomfortably and said, "I don't really understand it, but after he made me practice for some months, I found that when I concentrated in that way and then drew my gun or hit out at something, my hands moved at an unbelievable speed."

Beth said, "That's...that's..."

Jack laughed and said, "Unbelievable? If you had seen that Chinese man move, then you would have believed."

He suddenly stood up and pulled Beth up as well. "Let me show you something," he said. He gave her a coin and then moved back until he was five feet away from her.

"I want you to throw that coin at me," he said. "I don't mean just flip it, but throw it fast at me. Ready?" He held out his hands in front of him with the palms facing inward and said, "Now!"

Beth threw the coin, and Jack clapped his hands together. Beth said excitedly, "That was fast!" But Jack showed her his hands, which were empty, and then he bent, picked up the coin, and flipped it to her.

"That was my normal speed," he said. "I couldn't catch the coin, and it hit me on the chest and fell down."

He loosened his body in a series of small moves and then said, "I want you to count to ten in your mind and then throw the coin again. Make sure that you throw it real fast."

Beth counted to ten and then threw the coin with force at Jack. She hardly saw his hands move before she heard the clap of his palms meeting. He held his hands like that together and walked towards her. Slowly, he turned his palms upwards, and Beth saw the coin.

"You caught it," she said in an awed voice. "You actually caught it, and I threw it with such force!"

Jack smiled and said, "This time I did what the Chinese cook taught me. Whenever I am faced with trouble, I do what I learned from him, and that's why I am so fast."

They sat down again, and Beth asked him, "What's going to happen now, Jack?"

He looked at her for a moment without speaking and then

said, "Maybe this is as good a time as any to tell you. I'll be leaving in the morning before the break of dawn, and I won't be back for some time."

Beth cried out, "Jack, you can't leave! Please don't leave, Jack!"

He hugged her and said, "Maybe that came out the wrong way. I didn't mean I'm leaving the ranch or you folks. I'm just going hunting, and I won't be back until the hunt is over."

They stood up, and Beth asked, "What are you going to be hunting?"

Jack had turned to walk away and said over his shoulder, "Vermin! One in particular."

The next morning Jack was gone, and Ryan and Bruce were talking about it when Beth entered the dining room.

Ryan asked her, "Did Jack say anything to you, Beth? He hasn't come in for breakfast, and he isn't in his room. His warbag and his horse are also missing."

Beth said, "He told me that he's going hunting and that he won't be back until the hunt is over."

Bruce exclaimed, "Hunting? Hunting what?"

Beth said sadly, "Vermin, he said. One in particular." Then she sat down and started to cry.

Ryan rushed over and held her. "What's wrong, Beth?" he asked her. "Why the tears?"

Bruce sighed and told his father, "Come on, Dad! She's just in love, that's all!"

Ryan looked confused and asked, "In love? With whom…" His voice trailed off, and Bruce said, "Now you get it. Yes, she's in love with Jack. In fact, she's been in love with him since she was a kid, and she hasn't stopped."

Ryan said, "Well, I guess I can't complain about your choice in men. But I don't want to see you with a broken heart, Beth. What if he drifts again after all this is over?"

Bruce shrugged and said, "He won't, Dad, I can tell."

Beth looked up and asked him, "How can you be so sure?"

Bruce grimaced and said, "You must be blind. Can't you see that he's in love with you? When we rode in from town that first day and you were standing in the doorway? Old Jack was struck by a thunderbolt! It was so obvious!"

Beth stammered, "But...but...he hasn't said anything..."

Bruce sighed and told her, "And he won't because he is such a taciturn man who always finds it difficult to talk. You are going to have to tell him that you love him and not wait for him to tell you."

Suddenly Beth's face changed, and a knowing look spread over it as she said with a half-smile, "Well, Bruce, this may surprise you, but he isn't as taciturn as you think!" On that note, she got up and walked away, still smiling to herself.

Bruce gave Ryan a confused look and said, "Now what did she mean by that?"

Ryan laughed and told him, "Never underestimate a woman, my son. I learned that from your mother. I'd say that Jack talks to her a lot, and she's just realized what that means!"

Bruce suddenly turned serious and asked him, "What did Jack mean by one vermin in particular, Dad?"

Ryan sighed and said, "He's going hunting Black Wind. Mike said that he told him about Matt Duncan and Black Wind. I guess he's decided not to wait for Black Wind to start hunting him."

It turned out that Ryan was right.

CHAPTER 13
BLACK WIND

JACK HAD LEFT THE HOUSE LONG BEFORE THE breaking of dawn. Silently he had saddled his horse, tied his warbag behind the saddle, and sheathed his rifle with his army telescope next to it. Tied to his saddle horn were many squares of sacking that he had cut the night before and tied in a bundle. He also wore his moccasins and not his usual boots. He had a bandolier of cartridges across his shoulder and two more boxes in his warbag. He had packed plenty of jerky and biscuits with some bacon and ham. He did not intend to visit the ranch or the town for supplies until his hunt had ended. He rode straight to the old Porter ranch, and from the side of a hill overlooking the ranch, he lay flat and studied the layout through his telescope. He waited as patiently as an Indian, but his patience was soon rewarded. An hour before the break of dawn, he saw a man saddling his horse. Soon the man rode from the ranch in the direction of the Double M. Jack mounted his horse and waited for the man to pass before he started to follow him. He knew that this man was Black Wind and that he had guessed right. Black Wind was hunting him.

After about two miles, he came to a rocky slope and drew

rein at the top. He wrapped the hooves of his horse in the pieces of sacking, and then unsheathing his rifle, he took careful aim and shot the horse that Black Wind rode. The horse dropped dead, but Black Wind had already left the saddle with his rifle in his hand as soon as the shot was fired. He lay still and did not move, but Jack wasn't fooled for a moment. Taking careful aim, he placed a bullet close to Black Wind's head. Black Wind shot upright and, in a zigzag run he headed for the nearest cover, which happened to be a rocky hillside like the one Jack was on. Jack moved back, and mounting his horse he took a roundabout route and circled back behind Black Wind. He came to a grove of trees, and dismounting, he tied his horse to a tree with a long enough lead so that the horse could graze as well as lie down without difficulty. Then he slung his warbag and canteen over his shoulder and began making his way cautiously back to where he was before.

He knew that Black Wind would have noted where the shots came from, and he would be heading there now to track the man who had shot at him. Jack also knew that Black Wind would find no tracks leaving the hillside thanks to the bits of sacking that he had tied to his horse's hooves. It was a game of outthinking and confusing your opponent, and Ned Falcon had taught Jack well. Jack reached the spot as the sky was lightening with predawn light, and sure enough, he found Black Wind searching the area for tracks. Jack silently approached him from behind, but Black Wind sensed him and suddenly spun around and dropped to the ground with his rifle held ready. But Jack was already hidden behind an outcrop of rock before Black Wind started to turn. The old scout had always taught Jack never to underestimate an opponent, and so Jack assumed that Black Wind would sense his presence because Jack could do the same.

Now, with his rifle pointing straight at Black Wind, who was out in the open, he said conversationally, "I would drop that rifle right now if you want to live. This here Henry is already cocked and ready. But you do what you have to do." Black Wind considered his chances of shooting and running for cover, but he couldn't get a shot at Jack, and all Jack had to do was pull the trigger. Slowly he lay the rifle on the ground, and just as slowly he stood up. "Now unbuckle your gun belt and let it drop," said Jack. Then, still in a conversational tone of voice, he added, "I have to warn you that I have an itchy trigger finger, and I never warn a man twice." Slowly, making no sudden moves, Black Wind unbuckled his gun belt and let it fall. "Now turn around and stand still with your hands behind your back." Black Wind complied, and Jack said, "Keep those hands behind your back and hold your right wrist with your left hand." Black Wind did as asked and at last spoke. "You sure you don't want me to put my hands up?" he asked. "Where you from, anyhow? Over here you raise your hands in surrender." As he was speaking, he was slowly releasing his wrist, but as his hands began to part, he felt the barrel of the Henry poking his back and he stood still. Jack had covered the ground between them in a silent rush, and now with the rifle in Black Wind's back, he reached up and drew an Arkansas toothpick from where it hung between Black Wind's shoulder blades. Then he stepped back and said, "Turn around."

Black Wind turned around and looked keenly at Jack in the gathering light. "You're not a cow nurse," he said. "They told me you was a drifting cow nurse." Jack shrugged and said, "Actually I am, but I'm also a hunter like you. If I had told you to raise your hands, this knife would have been flying at me in a flash." He threw the knife at Black Wind's feet, and in a flash of speed he drew his bowie from the sheath between his shoulder blades. Black Wind gave him a wry smile and remarked, "Birds of a feather, huh?" But Jack did not smile when he said, "No, we're not. You're a bushwhacker who wouldn't give your opponent a fair shake, and that's not me." Black Wind gave him a puzzled look and asked, "You're not going to shoot me?" Jack carefully laid his rifle down and then stepped forward until he was about three feet away. "I'm giving you what I said, a fair shake," he told him. "Pick up your knife and let's see if you are as good as they say you are." Black Wind stared at him and then bent slowly and picked up his knife. With a cruel smile, he said, "You just made the biggest mistake of your life, Mister. No one beats me with a knife!" Jack said softly, "I've heard that one before and I'll tell you a new one. There's always someone better."

He held his knife with the blade pointing forward between his thumb and forefinger, while Black Wind held his in a closed fist with the blade pointing downward. Jack was glad that he wore his moccasins, as high-heeled cowboy boots could turn on a stone and unbalance a fighter, whereas with moccasins, he could feel every stone on the ground. He always wore moccasins when he was hunting and tracking as it was the best for silent movement. It was also the best footwear in a knife fight. Black Wind was puzzled as Jack did not crouch or circle but slowly walked straight towards him. He did not have his knife hand held straight out in front of him either. Instead, his knife hand was hanging down but slightly ahead of his body. Black Wind was a veteran of many a knife fight, but he had never seen any knife fighter act like the man in front of him. He started to circle but realized that that wasn't possible because Jack was crowding him, and he was forced to move back. Suddenly he stopped, and as Jack came within striking distance, he unleashed a backhand slash with the point of the blade for Jack's belly. His knife never reached Jack, for in a blur of motion, Jack's knife rose up and across and slashed his wrist to the bone, and the knife fell from his nerveless hand. The Bowie was razor-sharp and a heavy knife, and it almost severed Black Wind's wrist completely. Black Wind stared stupidly at the blood pouring from his severed wrist, and then he fell to his knees and looked up at Jack. "How?" was all he said. Jack did not answer him but reached forward, removed his bandana, and tied a tight tourniquet just above his elbow. The blood started to slow, and Jack said, "Well, you won't die. I'll tie you to your saddle, and you can make your way back to town and get the Doc there to stitch you up." After sending Black Wind on his way, Jack went back for his horse. He mounted and rode to the Double M and reached the ranch just as the family was finishing breakfast.

They heard the walking horse, and Beth ran out of the house. As Jack swung down from the saddle, she ran straight and jumped into his arms. Jack held her and said softly, "You do know you're not eight years old anymore." She blushed as he set her down and then said, "Your hunt finished pretty fast." Jack shrugged and said, "I got lucky, I guess." Beth took his arm, and they walked towards the house. She said softly, "Somehow, I don't believe that luck had anything to do with it. Not where you are concerned." Jack looked down and gave her a thoughtful look but did not say anything. They sat on the porch and Ryan and Bruce joined them. Ryan said, "You went hunting Black Wind and I'm guessing you found him." It was a statement and not a question, and Jack said, "I went to the old Porter ranch as I figured he would make an early start. I was right, for Black Wind came out much before dawn and set out for the Double M. I guess I saved him the long ride." Bruce asked eagerly, "Is he dead?" Jack frowned and told him, "I taught you a long time ago that you kill only if you have to; and then you don't hesitate, or you're a dead man." Bruce looked shamefaced and said, "No, I didn't forget, Jack. I just figured that with his reputation, the only way to stop him would be to kill him." Jack smiled and told him, "It's okay, kid, I know what you meant. You see, he thought he was after a drifting cowboy, and so he didn't take precautions. If he had known that I was also a hunter, then this encounter would not have ended so fast. But no, Bruce, I didn't kill him. I just tied him to his horse and sent him on his way to town to see the Doc." But Bruce couldn't leave it and wanted to know, so he asked, "You shot him? You done beat him at his own game?" Jack sighed and told him, "No, I didn't shoot him, but I guess he won't be using his knife any time soon."

Changing the subject, Jack asked Ryan, "So what have you and the Baileys decided to do?"

"Well," explained Ryan. "We figured that Dan White will be like a mad bull right now, what with all the whittling down that you've been doing, and it's likely that he'll want to bring the fight to us. I'm guessing that he is going to make an all-out attack to once and for all finish the lot of us." Jack nodded and said, "Makes sense, I reckon. So what do you folks plan on doing?" Ryan told him, "The Double M is easier to defend than the Rafter K. This house is up against the hillside, and two men on that ridge behind us with rifles can easily dissuade anyone who tries attacking from there. They can approach only from the front, and we can see them coming a long ways off, as it's mostly open grassland with sparse tree cover. So the Baileys are coming over here this morning, and they'll stay here until this is over." He looked at Jack for approval and added, "We'll be ready for them when they do come. You agree, Jack?" Jack nodded in agreement and said, "Sure, that sounds like a right good plan."

Ryan gave him a searching look and said, "But you are thinking of doing something else." When Jack just shrugged, Ryan added, "I know you, Jack, and I know when you're agreeing but have something else planned. So what is it?" Jack looked at him thoughtfully and then said, "Well, the way I figure it, Dan White is a dangerous man and can threaten everyone here only because he has a bunch of hired guns at his back. That's been my thinking right from the start. Now he doesn't have as many hired guns as he once did." Bruce said, "But he still has Matt Duncan, and Nat Hardy is still around. Hardy must be desperate for revenge to gain back his reputation that you tore to smithereens." Ryan said, "That makes him more dangerous because he would rather die than leave here without getting his revenge. And Dan White still has a dozen or more hired guns at his back to do his bidding." Jack said, "I know that, but if the big guns are taken out, then the others will tend to look at their hole card. These are men who fight for wages and not honor or loyalty, so when they see the tide turn against them with the elimination of their top guns, then they tend to drift. I've seen it happen before, as hired guns will fight only when the odds are in their favor. I intend to change those odds." Ryan told him, "There are two things wrong with that plan, son. One, you're obviously better than Black Wind, and so you can do what he was hired for. You could hunt them all down and kill them, and they wouldn't stand a chance against you; but you won't do that because you're not like Black Wind. Two, you intend to go to town and face them down in a fair fight. Only there won't be any fair fight, because they'll be waiting for you, and a dozen guns are just too many guns."

CHAPTER 14
WAR TALK

JACK HAD BEEN STARING INTO THE DISTANCE AT A cloud of approaching dust, and now he smiled and said, "Well, it looks like I've got two more guns to whittle down those dozen." They all stood up, and Jack walked into the yard and waited for the horses to come in. Two men rode into the yard and swung down from their saddles. Ryan gasped and shouted, "Well, I'll be damned! Jason Montana and Poco Pete!" The two men looked up, and Jason said, "Good to see you, Ryan. And you two must be Bruce and Beth?" He laughed, and walking up to Jack, he pumped his hand hard and said, "I got the word that the Double M was in trouble and you wanted me here like yesterday, so I rounded up Poco Pete and we rode two pairs of horses to a standstill to get here as fast as we could." Then he gave Jack a mock frown and growled, "And if you tell me that you've already had all the fun, then I'll be mighty sore with you!" Jack smiled and said, "Don't worry, Jase, there's plenty of trouble to go around." Poco Pete came up, shook his hand, and said, "I ran into Pike Roland when I got the word from Jase, and I told him that you were facing some trouble. He's rounding up some of our old unit, and I expect he'll be here with at least five of them within the week."

They were all seated, talking about old times and old friends on the Double M, when the Bailey family rode up. Jack performed the introductions, and Ryan told old man Bailey what Jack was proposing to do. He also said that at least six more men from Jack's army unit should be arriving within a week. Old man Bailey said, "I have no doubt that they are good soldiers, but what could they do against the likes of Matt Duncan and Nat Hardy? This is our fight, and me and the boys will go with Jack to town. No need to put anyone else in danger." Mike said to no one in particular, "When I was in the cavalry, I heard tell that Major Donovan's men would stand and die for him if he so wished." They all stared at him, and he added, "It's also a fact that Major Donovan's unit was the best raiding company in the whole Confederate army." He looked at Jason Montana and said, "I reckon you were his hell-for-leather Captain? You fit the description anyway." Jason laughed and declared, "Sure I was, and I am, and proud to be at his side anytime at all." Old man Bailey said by way of explanation, "Mike and Brian joined up. I figured sending two of my sons to fight was enough, and the others were too young anyways." Ryan remarked, "We've all heard of Major Donovan and his company and what they achieved; I just never made the connection. I must be the dumbest fool in the world!" Brian said, "Well, to be fair, he was only known as Major Donovan with no first name, and it took the two of us some time to figure it out ourselves. You see, during the war, he was always a shadowy figure and refused to come into the light. Word was that he even refused a bunch of commendations and medals, so hardly anyone knew what he looked like or who he actually was." Jack said, with a half-smile playing around his mouth, "Rumors can exaggerate events, for we took our losses like every other unit. But having said that, the ones that remain are the best, and I would storm hell with them at my back anytime at all!"

"So are we all agreed?" asked old man Bailey. "We ride for town tomorrow?" There was some perceptible hesitation, and everyone looked at each other to see how the land lay.

It was Mark, who never usually spoke during any discussion, who now said conversationally, "Was it me in Dan White's boots at the moment, I know what I would do." Everyone looked at him and old man Bailey said, "Spit it out, son." Mark shrugged and said, "Well, I would think that with you all hunkered down here waiting for me to strike, I would just sneak in with my men and drive off with your herds of cattle." They all just stared at him, and suddenly Jack swore, and jumping up, he raced for his horse. Right on his heels were Jason, Poco Pete, Mike, and Brian. Luke had started out after them, but Mark said, "Stay here, Luke!" Luke turned around, and by way of explanation, Mark added, "I could be wrong about the herd, and they could make a sneak attack here. Besides, I reckon those five can handle anything that Dan White throws at them." Old man Bailey told Ryan, "Mark rarely has anything to say, but when he does, we've all learned to listen to him."

Jack and the others rode hard and fast to where the cattle usually were to be found at this time. As they rode, at Jack's command, they spread out so that there was at least a 100 feet between any two riders. Soon they heard the bellow of cattle and rode harder until they could see riders, rounding up the cattle in bunches, and driving them to what seemed to be the gathering ground straight ahead. Mike went after three men who were herding a small bunch of steers, and Brian swung to join up with him. Off to the other side were four more riders rounding up cattle, and straight ahead there were five more trying to keep the herd together. Jack shouted, "Jase, Pete, go get those four over there and I'll take the ones with the herd." Jason and Poco Pete swung away, while Jack rode straight ahead.

Mike and Brian rode hard until they were in rifle range, and then they pulled their rifles and slowed their horses. Riding easily in the saddle, they took aim and fired, and two of the riders dropped from their horses. The third swung around on seeing the two approaching riders and the empty saddles of his companions' horses and rode for the gathering ground. Mike swung down from his saddle on the run, and dropping to the ground on one knee, he took careful aim and fired, and the rider seemed to fling up his arms and drop to the ground. Brian had not stopped but had gone on and caught the reins of Mike's horse, and now he rode back and threw the reins to Mike, who caught them and swung back into the saddle. They looked around, and not seeing any other riders, they rode for the gathering ground.

Jason and Poco Pete rode fast, and when they were in rifle range, Poco Pete drew his rifle, and dropping to the ground on one knee, he fired in one smooth movement and emptied a saddle, while Jason continued to race ahead. The other three riders, seeing a lone man coming up on them, charged straight at Jason, drawing their pistols as they rode. They fired and missed, but Jason continued to ride until he was closer, and then suddenly his hand dipped and in one smooth movement his pistol came up and two shots rang out. Two of the riders were flung from their saddles, and then a rifle shot sounded from Poco Pete and the last rider was thrown from his horse.

Jack raced his horse straight ahead, and the riders with the herd saw him coming. They looked left and right and saw the others riding away and Jack approaching them alone. They rode forward with rifles drawn to meet Jack and started firing before they were in range. Jack drew his rifle, and slowing his horse, he began shooting. His hand was a blur of motion as he repeatedly worked the lever action and fired. Although he was mounted and his targets were also riding, he still emptied the five saddles in less than a minute. The sound of rapid gunfire had spooked the small herd and they had begun to stampede, but Jack rode fast around the herd until he overtook it and then started firing his rifle into the air from the side of the herd in an effort to turn the running cattle. From his right came Jason and Poco Pete riding hard for the point and firing into the ground in front of the lead steer. From the left came Mike and Brian, firing their rifles in the air and whooping and screaming. Gradually, the herd started to turn, and soon they were running towards the Double M range instead of away from it.

Satisfied that the cattle would soon get tired and stop, Jack and the others pulled up and slowly rode back to where the rustlers had fallen. The three that Mike and Brian had shot were unrecognizable as human beings as the turning herd had run right over them and their bodies were trampled into the mud. They rode to the gathering ground and found two of the five that Jack had taken on still alive. Mike and Brian dropped to the ground to tend to them, while the rest rode on to where Jason and Poco Pete had dropped the other four riders. After a cursory examination, Poco Pete declared, "These have gone to meet their Maker." They rode back to join Mike and Brian and found that they had bandaged the wounds of the two rustlers. Mike said, "This one will be okay, the bullet missed his heart and his lungs, but the other is shot through the lung." Jack said, "Put them on their horses, and that man can take his sidekick to town. We had better make a sweep of the range and then head to the ranch house." Mike said, "What about the dead ones?" Jack told him, "We'll send some hands to bury them, but right now we need to move. We'll split up: Pete and Jason, you cover the western range; Mike and Brian, you take the eastern, and I'll check straight ahead. Make it a fast sweep, boys, and if you don't see anyone after a hundred yards, then swing back to the ranch house. And if anyone runs into trouble, the signal will be three rapid shots and the rest of us will come a-running. Let's move!"

They were all gathered in the yard of the ranch house. They had not seen any more rustlers, and they figured that the twelve they had seen were it. Ryan said, "But if you've taken out twelve, then that leaves Dan White with how many guns now?" It was Mike who answered, "I'd say he still has plenty." He told Jack, "Maybe two of those men were part of the fifteen hired guns I told you about. The rest were new, I hadn't seen any of them before." Jack nodded his head thoughtfully and said, "So he's been hiring still, which means he intended to make a clean sweep just as we thought." Old man Bailey said, "Our five hands are holed up in our ranch house, and they'll defend it if attacked. Ryan has ten hands here to hold this place, so I say we go with Jack's plan and the rest of us ride into town. Let's end this fight right now!" Ryan demurred, "Sure, I can hold this place with my cowboys; half of them will fort up in the bunkhouse, and the rest will be with us here. As you can see, the bunkhouse is at right angles to the ranch house, and we can cover most of the ground. But who knows how many men Dan White has hired? You ride into town now, and you could be riding into a small army for all we know!" Mike said, "Pa, maybe we shouldn't split up our forces. In fact, maybe we should send a few men to strengthen the defense of our place. Those five wouldn't hold up for long if Dan White attacks in force."

They all started talking at the same time until Jack said, and this was Major Donovan speaking, "Enough! I agree with Mike. Ryan, pick out five of your best and send them to the Rafter K. That will leave you with five, and the Baileys, which makes ten; plus there's you, Bruce, and the two young ladies. Just fort up well and stay put." Mike said, "Which leaves you, Jason, and Pete. No way you're riding to town without me, Major!" Jack sighed and told him, "Mike, I'd be proud to have you at my side, but think of this as a military operation. If they come in strength, then you are the one with the army experience to plan and hold them off; it's what we've grown used to. We're not going to town painted for war, we're going to sneak in and sneak out just to find out how many men Dan White has with him." Mike stared at him for a moment and then sighed and nodded his head. "Okay, I'll buy that, but I still don't like it!" he said. Before anyone could come up with any more objections, Jack said, "Let's go, boys!" He, Jason, and Poco Pete swiftly mounted their horses and rode away at a fast trot. Watching them go, Mike said, "You know, he makes sense at that. Ryan, you pick out four of your men, and Brian here will go with them. If they do attack our place in force, then Brian should be there. Jack is right; we do have the experience of fighting against a larger force. For the last two years of the war, that seems to be all that we did!"

While Ryan was picking out four cowboys to ride with Brian, Mike went to the bunkhouse and came out with two spades and some sticks of wood. He threw a spade to Brian, and the two of them began pacing off from the front of the bunkhouse and the ranch house respectively. Bruce ran up, and taking the sticks from Mike, he asked, "You're marking out a firing range? That's smart!" Mike shrugged, "It's what we did in the war. Helped us to save our ammunition, and we never had enough of that anyway!" They marked the distance for pistol range and also for rifle range and drove in the sticks as markers. The ranch hands came up, and Mike explained to them what they were doing. Then he studied the approaches to the ranch house and asked Ryan if he had any explosives. "We have some dynamite left. We used it to blast the rocks from the new field where we planted our alfalfa."

"Be obliged if you'd get them and enough fuse wire as well," Mike told him. The four brothers and Bruce walked out for some distance and then split up to cover a circle around the ranch house and bunkhouse. Spacing out the distance, they dug shallow holes in the ground, placed the dynamite with care, and covered it with loose sand. They trailed the fuses to the ranch house and then covered them also with loose sand. After they had finished, Brian and four cowboys left for the Rafter K, taking with them the remaining dynamite sticks. Ryan told old man Bailey, "It looks like your boys have a lot of experience in waging war!" Nolan Bailey shrugged and said simply, "I guess you could say that is true for all of us. We've had our share of troubles and we came here to find peace. But trouble just seems to follow us!"

CHAPTER 15
THE BAILEYS

NOLAN BAILEY CAME FROM A FEUDING CLAN IN Tennessee. His family had a long-running feud with the Hawkes clan, and when Nolan turned seventeen he met and fell in love with Kate Hawkes. They tried their best to keep their love a secret because they knew that their families would never agree to it. But love cannot be hidden for long, and one day two of Kate's cousins braced Nolan in the hills. He shot and killed both of them, but they got two bullets into him before they died. It took him a month to recover from his wounds, and then he and Kate went down to the flatlands and found a preacher to marry them. Strangely enough, after their marriage, the feud between the families died down; and while they never became friends, at least they stopped killing each other.

Nolan and Kate struggled to raise their five children on their small farm, and Nolan used to go west for months at a time to trap for furs and to hunt buffalo for the hides. When Mike turned sixteen, the entire family migrated westwards. They settled on a farm in Kansas, but two years of drought left them with nothing and they moved to Colorado. All the children were taught at an early age to handle firearms, and Mike and Brian became expert sharpshooters with a rifle. Brian was faster in drawing his pistol and accurate in his shooting. But it was Mark who later became the fastest gun in the family. However, the family's first choice of weapon was always the rifle, and they were all experts in its use.

In Kansas, they had started well and had got their first crop in, and Nolan was cautiously optimistic about the future. A war had started between two big ranches, and everyone began taking sides, but the Baileys stayed out of it. The Bar T was owned by Sean Travis, and he was a decent, hard-working man who had come up the hard way. The Rocking R was owned by Ray Rayburn, who had bought the ranch from the previous owner. A good-sized stream ran through the area where the boundaries of the two ranches met. Sean Travis and the previous owner of the present Rocking R had settled the issue amicably by agreeing that both ranches could use the water, and the stream was declared common ground. When Rayburn bought the ranch, he declared that the stream belonged to him and that the Bar T cattle could not use the water. Rayburn fancied himself as a fast gun, and he had brought in a tough crew to run the ranch. A Bar T cowboy was shot dead when he was crossing the stream, and in retaliation, the Bar T crew shot dead two hands of the Rocking R. Both ranches dug trenches and put up ramparts on their side of the stream, and anyone approaching the stream was shot at. Rayburn soon began importing hired guns, and they took over the town of Ashgrove to prevent the Bar T from getting their supplies there.

One day Kate and Mike had gone to town to stock up on supplies. They had loaded the wagon, and Kate was in the driver's seat. Mike had mounted his horse and they were about to move out when two of Rayburn's hired guns came out of the saloon and walked towards them.

"Hey!" one of them shouted. "Hold up there! No one can get supplies from this town."

Kate told them, "We own a small farm and we're not involved in this fight between the two ranches."

One of the men sneered and said, "How do we know that's true? You might be selling those supplies to the Bar T!"

The other man sniggered, "Maybe she's selling more than just supplies!"

In a flash, Mike was off his horse and facing the two men. "That's my mother," he said. "Apologize or die; your choice!"

The two men laughed, and one of them said, "You ain't dry behind the ears yet, kid!"

The other man said, "But since you want to die, you can!"

They went for their guns, and Mike gunned them down. He swung into his saddle, and he and Kate drove back to the farm.

The next day word reached them that Rayburn had told his men to shoot them on sight. Nolan's code had always been to face trouble head-on, and his boys were the same. So he, Mike, and Brian belted on their guns, and with their rifles in hand they rode for the Rocking R. Brian was just fourteen at the time, but a man grown with a rifle in his hands, and he was fast on the draw as well. They reined in their horses in a grove of trees about 30 yards from the ranch house and waited in the shelter of the trees with their rifles held ready. Four men came out of the bunkhouse, and the four men died before they had taken more than three steps. The Baileys did not believe in fair warnings when hired guns were given orders to shoot them on sight. Nolan had taught his children that whether on four legs or two, vermin were just vermin, and you shot them where you saw them.

The rifle shots brought out more men from the bunkhouse and the ranch house. The Baileys kept up a steady fire, and three more men died before the rest realized what was happening and ran for shelter. They started shooting towards the trees from the bunkhouse and the ranch house, but the Baileys didn't return their fire. They were not taught to waste bullets, and they just waited for a target to show before shooting. Mike circled around and came up at the back of the bunkhouse. He moved silently closer and set two fires next to the wall of the bunkhouse. Then he circled again to the side of the ranch house, where he again set two fires, and then circled back to where his brother and father waited. The defenders only realized what was happening when the log walls started burning.

"Hey!" a man shouted from the bunkhouse. "There ain't enough water here to put out the fire. You ain't going to let us burn here, are you?"

Nolan shouted back, "Throw out your guns and come out with your hands empty, and you can live."

There was silence for a moment, and then guns were thrown out the door and men came out from the bunkhouse and the ranch house with their hands held high.

Nolan said, "Which one of you is Rayburn?"

A tall man with a low-slung tied-down empty holster said, "That's me, and you'll pay for this!"

Nolan and Brian stepped out from behind the trees, while Mike stayed in cover. Nolan told Rayburn, "You put out the word that your hired guns would shoot us down on sight. I'm giving you a fair chance to back up your words with action. Pick up your gun and holster it. This young son of mine will take you on."

Rayburn looked at the gangling youth and laughed. "This will be a pleasure," he said.

He picked up his pistol, dropped it in his holster, and then went into a crouch. As soon as his gun was in the holster and he went into the gunman's crouch, Brian drew and fired. It was sudden and it was fast, and maybe Rayburn was expecting some talk first, but if so, he was mistaken. The first thing that Nolan had taught his children was simply this: "If you're going to shoot, then don't wait around for the sun to set. Just shoot!" Rayburn died there in front of his burning ranch house, and the war between the ranches ended. Two years later, the Baileys moved again after drought defeated them.

In Colorado, the Baileys started to prosper and grow when they took to raising cattle, but rustlers and an extremely cold winter wiped them out. Mike and Brian had taken out after the rustlers, and in a shootout they killed four of them, but they could not shoot their way out of the worst winter in many years that hit Colorado. They were broke with no money to restock their ranch, so they left Colorado and moved to Gila City, Arizona to mine gold and raise a stake for their future. They staked out claims and worked hard during the gold rush, and got together a nice stake to start their own ranch. With money in their pockets, the family sat down and discussed their next move. They decided against going back to Colorado. They had heard of the cattle ranches in Texas, and so the decision was made to settle in Texas and start ranching in a big way. Nolan went ahead to find a place, and the family followed with a herd of cattle. But on the way to Texas, they were attacked by an Apache war party, and while they succeeded in saving the herd and driving back the Indians, Kate Bailey was killed by an Apache arrow. They named their ranch in Texas the Rafter K in honor of Kate.

CHAPTER 16
MATT DUNCAN

JACK, JASON, AND POCO PETE WENT FIRST TO THE OLD Porter ranch and from the hillside Jack studied the ranch and its surroundings. Men came and went from the bunkhouse to the main house and after an hour Jack said, "I figure there are around a dozen men down there." He got up and went to his horse and said over his shoulder, "Let's enter town from the other direction." They rode in a wide circle so that they approached the town from the east. They didn't ride down the main street but rode along the back of the town's buildings. They walked their horses and glanced in at the buildings that they passed. They were keeping a tally of the men in town, and when they reached the First Chance Saloon they drew up and Jack said, "I make it around fifty men, ten of whom I would say are Dan White's hired guns who are here in the saloon right now." Jason agreed and said, "I made it a dozen of his men so far scattered in the other saloons."

"Pete, we'll hitch our horses here and you check that the back door is clear," said Jack. "Then you take position at that side window. Keep out of sight but make sure that you can see what's going down in the saloon. Once we start the party, make sure to join in, but not before. Jason and me, we'll walk through the front door, but most probably we'll be leaving through the back." Pete nodded and Jason asked, "Pistols or rifles, Jack?" Jack jerked his rifle from his horse and said, "Both. Likely we'll need them." They held the rifles with their left hands with a finger on the trigger. Both of them could shoot left-handed with a rifle and with good accuracy as well. Jason had been taught by Jack during the war and he was faster now on the draw than he had ever been. Although he and Poco Pete would never admit to it, they both hero-worshipped Jack and would follow him into hell willingly.

Jack and Jason walked softly around the building, and then stepping onto the boardwalk, they walked casually up to the front door. Halting at the batwings, they quickly scanned the room and Jack said, "I make it around ten guns. You go left and I'll go right, and we don't waste any time." Although Jack had told Ryan and Mike that they were just going to sneak in and sneak out after figuring out how many men Dan White had, they never intended to do that. Jack's plan was always to whittle down the opposition and that's what he intended to do now, which was the reason why he didn't want Mike along. He thought that Mike might hesitate at the wrong moment when it came to shooting, but Jason and Pete never would. During the war, Jack's unit was famous for sneaking into a Yankee encampment and then suddenly opening fire. By the time the Yankees figured out what was happening and tried to shoot back, there was no one to shoot at. Jack's unit would just vanish like a wisp of smoke in the night. Jack had just met the Baileys, so he wasn't to know until later just how mistaken he was in that judgment, because the Baileys would never hesitate when it came to shooting.

Jack pushed apart the batwing doors and he and Jason

walked in. He went right and Jason went left and then Jack addressed the room, saying, "If you're Dan White's hired guns, drop your gun belts right now and live. If you're not, then leave through the back door right now!" There was an immediate rush as the townsfolk left through the back door, leaving ten men standing in the saloon. Six of them were at the bar while four of them sat at a table playing cards by the side window. One of the men at the bar laughed, "You're not serious, are you? Two of you are going to take on ten of us?" As he spoke, everyone went for their guns and the room was soon filled with gunsmoke. Jason shot all three on his side with his pistol. Jack did the same with the three in front of him and then swung his rifle one-handedly and shot one of the men at the table who was lifting his gun to shoot. The other three men at the table had already been shot by Poco Pete with his rifle through the window. Jack and Jason then coolly walked through the room and out the back door where all three swung into their saddles and trotted their horses until they had left the town, and then they went into a fast gallop heading for the old Porter ranch.

From the hillside overlooking the ranch house, Jack searched the area with his telescope. He soon discovered that there were a lot of horses missing from the remuda. "Looks like they're hitting the ranches," Jack said. "Let's go then," said Jason, heading for his horse. "Hold on, Jase," Jack told him. "They're not going to surprise the folks at the ranch since we were expecting an attack." Jason frowned, "So what's the plan?" Jack folded the telescope and headed for his horse. "Why, I was thinking that we might ease on down to that there ranch and see just how many gunslingers are there now." Jason grinned and they all mounted up and slowly walked their horses down the hillside to the house. The ranch house was silent, but there was movement and sound from the bunkhouse. Jack told Poco Pete, "Stand at the side of the house and keep a watch on the front door. Me and Jase will visit the bunkhouse." They tied the horses to a tree and walked the rest of the way on foot. Poco Pete took up station by the house and Jack and Jason eased up to the door of the bunkhouse, which was open. Loosening their guns in their holsters and with their rifles in their left hands, they casually walked into the bunkhouse and moved apart.

They counted six men all told, two were lying on their bunks and four men were playing cards at a table. For a moment no one seemed to notice them and then one of the men who was lying down sat up abruptly and shouted, "What the hell?" The rest became aware of the intruders, and they all stared at them. The four at the table started to rise but the two rifles were pointed in their direction and Jack said, "Was I you, I'd just sit tight, because at this range we don't miss our shots, but you do what you want to do." The men subsided, but the other man who was lying down got up slowly from his bunk and faced them. His hand hovered over his pistol and he said softly, "At this range, I don't miss either, and I'm betting that I can take the both of you before you can turn those rifles on me. The name's Matt Duncan, but think on this, by turning the rifles on me you leave yourselves open to those four yahoos at the table." Instead of talking, Jack drew in a blazing flash of speed and his pistol was pointing at Matt when he said, "Well, I guess I don't really need to turn my rifle. I'd be obliged if you men would just drop your gun belts right now." He paused and no one moved, so he added, "Or you can keep them, and we'll just put a bullet in you." He pulled back the hammer of his pistol and said, "The rifles are cocked and now so is my pistol." Jason said, "Same here, and I'm only counting to three before I fire. One, two..." The men hastily unbuckled and let their gun belts drop, all except for Matt Duncan who still stood there staring at Jack. Jack sighed and asked him, "You want to brace me?" Duncan said, "Let's see how good you are when you don't have the drop." Jack nodded his head and said, "All you men turn around and line up." They did, and Jason went and tied their hands behind their backs and then herded them out of the bunkhouse. Jack looked at Matt Duncan and said politely, "After you."

When they were all outside in the open, Jack asked Matt, "Anyone in the house?" Duncan shook his head, "They're gone raiding. I got back after they had left, which is why I'm still here." Jack said, "Pete, check out the house, and if there is even a single person there, then I'll put a bullet in Duncan's head." Pete went into the house, and after a while he came out and said, "It's empty." Jack told him, "You and Jason watch these rannies and keep an eye out for any approaching dust." He handed his rifle to Poco Pete and then faced Matt Duncan. "Okay," he said. "You got your wish." Duncan went into the gunfighter's crouch with his hand hovering over his gun butt, but Jack just stood there with his hand near his gun. Suddenly in a flash of speed Duncan drew and a shot rang out and the gun dropped from his hand. There was an audible sigh from the bound men and Matt Duncan stared stupidly at his empty hand. He had been shot through the wrist which had caused his gun to drop out of his hand just as he drew it. Jack turned to the other hired guns and said, "You men have a choice. Mount up and ride out and don't stop until you're out of Texas, or stay and we shoot it out right here and right now. Cut their hands loose, Pete." With their hands free, one of the men told Jack, "Mister, if it's all the same to you, we'll ride out." Another man asked him, "Why didn't you just kill Duncan? Why the fancy shooting?" Jack shrugged and replied, "A man once told me to kill only when necessary." The man shook his head in wonder and said, "And it wasn't necessary to kill Matt Duncan! Mister, that's a story that's going to keep a lot of campfires burning!" They did the best they could with Duncan's wrist and then they all mounted up and rode away. Jason asked Jack, "Now we ride for the ranch?" Jack pondered and then said, "Burn the house and the bunkhouse and we'll take the horses with us." Jason looked at him and said, "Jack, you do know that the war is over?" But Jack told him, "Jase, this is just another war and they brought it to us. I intend to leave them with no war headquarters." Jason lifted his hand and said, "Yo! I got it, Major. Pete, let's burn it!"

CHAPTER 17
THE CEDAR CREEK BATTLE

DAN WHITE LED THE ATTACK ON THE DOUBLE M ranch house with 20 hired gunfighters. Nat Hardy led the attack on the Rafter K with 15 men. Nat Hardy had definitely become unstable after the slapping meted out by Jack at the Double M. He would ignore the talk around him and would appear to be immersed in his own thoughts, but suddenly he would erupt at the slightest provocation. He had killed two of the hired guns in a manic eruption of rage when he thought that they were laughing at him, and everyone walked softly around him now. Dan White had wanted to keep him close and had included him in his group, but Hardy had insisted on leading the attack on the Rafter K, and Dan White had given in.

Dan White was an angry man but also a worried one, because for the first time he was doubting his ability to take over the two ranches. Just this morning, the team of a dozen men he had sent to rustle the cattle of the two ranches had not returned, and he feared that they were dead. Luckily, he had already sent for more hired guns, and they had arrived just in time. He was riding now as he had decided that with one full frontal assault, he would wipe out both ranches and bring this thing to an end. It was a sudden decision, and that was why Matt Duncan wasn't in the attacking force, as he had just arrived with another six hired guns. Dan White thought of all this as he rode and a chill went up his spine as he thought about this stranger called Jack Donovan. Who the hell was he, and where did he suddenly appear from? Undoubtedly he was a gunfighter, as he had taken down Leon Mendoza in a fair fight.

They were nearing the ranch house as the gloom of dusk was setting in, and he gave the order to slow down. The cavalcade slowed to a trot and then split into two groups, one group heading at an angle for the bunkhouse and the other riding at an angle for the ranch house. The plan was to approach both buildings from the side and not from the front. An attack from the rear was out of the question, as they were aware of the fact that just one rifle could keep the attackers pinned on the hillside; therefore, an attack from the side of the buildings was decided upon. There was absolutely no movement from either building, and Dan White began to feel uneasy. It was too calm and too quiet with no one to be seen, and his inbuilt sense of danger began to tingle. He slowly but unobtrusively began to drop back and let the others take the lead. The horses now slowed to a walk as they neared the buildings, and the men held their guns at the ready for quick action.

As they neared the buildings, both groups started to spread out a bit and slowed their approach even more. Suddenly there were loud explosions, one after another, and men and horses were flying through the air and falling. There was utter pandemonium, with horses whinnying shrilly and men swearing and shouting. There was dust and debris flying everywhere, and it looked to Dan White like a scene from hell. He had fallen to the rear of the group, and because of that, he had just barely escaped the force of the explosions. His horse reared up and whinnied as a man's bloody hand fell directly in front of it. Dan White looked around wildly and could see men fallen everywhere and bits and pieces of what looked like the remains of men and horses. Before the dust could settle, there was a volley of rifle fire from both buildings and more of his men fell dead or wounded. The ones that were left had had enough, and their horses were spooked anyway, so they turned and rode fast and hard away from the ranch. In a daze, Dan White turned his horse and rode hard for the Porter ranch. In his confused mind, one thought kept running: he would pick up Matt Duncan and the remaining hired guns, and he would come right back and attack the ranch again, and this time he would succeed. He was Dan White after all, pirate and smuggler, and he never failed.

At the Rafter K, the outcome of the attack by Nat Hardy was almost the same. Nat Hardy did not bother about stealth; instead, he and his group rode hard for the front of the ranch house. Nat Hardy was yards ahead of the rest when the explosions happened, and so he escaped the worst of the blasts, although he was thrown from his horse, hit his head on a stone, and lay half-dazed on the ground. In a repeat of the defense of the Double M, after the blasts there was a sustained volley of gunfire from the ranch house, and the few attackers who were left turned tail and raced their horses away from the ranch. Brian and some of the ranch hands came out with their rifles held ready, but all they found were dead bodies and a few badly wounded men and horses. They put the horses out of their misery and picked up the wounded, bringing them to the front yard of the ranch house. Brian was just laying a man down when he saw a figure start to rise up from the corner of his eye, and he turned around swiftly. The man stood up, and Brian saw that it was Nat Hardy; but a Nat Hardy with blood all over his face from a cut on his head and wild eyes that stared at Brian. His mouth worked, but no words could be heard, and Brian said, "It's over, Hardy, just drop your gun and settle down right there!" Suddenly Nat Hardy found his voice, and he screamed, "I'll kill you!" He drew his gun in a flashing draw, but no man lived who could beat the speed of a Henry bullet. Brian just tilted the barrel of his rifle and shot Hardy straight through the heart. As Nat Hardy fell dead, Brian muttered, "I guess ole Jack really did slap all the sense out of you!" Then he turned around and told three of his ranch hands, "See what you can do for these wounded but make it fast. Put them on their horses and send them on their way, and then stay put here in the house. Me and the others are riding to the Double M."

They arrived at the Double M ranch house at the same time as Jack and the others. Jack surveyed the carnage and said, "Man! This was a slaughter! Any sign of Dan White?" Old man Bailey said, "I think he was right at the back of the group, and he turned his horse and hightailed it. Leastwise, I'm pretty sure that was him." Jack asked Brian, "How did it go at the Rafter K?" Brian shrugged, "The same as here. They just weren't expecting something like this. Although they should have, since they came painted for war! Nat Hardy led the group, and he was knocked down by the explosion and cracked his head on the ground, I reckon. After it was over and the survivors had fled, he suddenly stood up and drew on me." Mike said, "Well, you're still standing." Brian shrugged, "I had me my rifle in my hands and aimed at him, but the man was fool enough to think that he could draw faster than a Henry bullet."

Ryan asked Jack, "You think Dan White's headed back to his ranch to bring more men? Or will he lay low for a while now?" Jack said, "Well, he doesn't have a ranch to go to, we burned it to the ground. So my guess would be that when he sees the burned-down ranch house, he'll ride to town. There may be about another dozen of his hired guns in town." Poco Pete said, "There were another ten, but we kind-a whittled them down, so yes, there should be a dozen left or thereabouts." Luke asked Brian, "But where's Matt Duncan? Was he in the group that attacked you? He sure wasn't in this group here." Brian just shook his head, and it was Jason who answered. "Matt Duncan has just left Texas with about six hired guns," he said. "Guess he didn't like the climate!"

"Yeah!" chimed in Poco Pete. "He didn't like the wind whistling through the hole in his wrist!" There was a clamor with everyone asking what had happened, so Jason held up his hand and said, "Slow down folks, and I'll tell you a tale, a tale that will keep many a campfire burning, as one of those hired guns who just left with Duncan said!" He then related the sequence of events as it had unfolded and ended with, "One of those hired guns asked Jack why he didn't kill Duncan, and Jack said that a man once told him to only kill when necessary! That threw them, I can tell you! It wasn't necessary to kill Matt Duncan, as Jack could just as easily shoot him in the wrist!"

Jack was fidgeting while Jason was talking, and now he said, "Okay, you've told your tale, Jase, now let's get down to the here and now! We know that Dan White only has the dozen or so men that we saw in town. By now, they know about what happened to the ten guns in the First Chance Saloon, and my guess is that some of them would have drifted out of town by now. Hired guns won't like it that three men rode into town and took out ten of their number. Those are odds most of them will find hard to live with, so they'll drift." Mike said, "So you're saying we finish it?" Jack nodded and said, "We finish it right now, tonight, before Dan White can bring in any more guns!" Old man Bailey said, "Enough talking, let's ride!" Jack held up his hand and said, "Wait a bit! No need for all of us to ride to town. Just to be on the safe side, we should leave enough people to defend the ranch as well. There's me, Jase, and Pete; with your boys, that makes seven, which is more than enough to handle whatever there is in town. You folks stay put here, we'll be back in no time." Mike said, "He's right, Pa, we can handle what's left of Dan White's army."

And so they rode to town, seven strong. They were young men in years but old in experience. They rode not with bravado but with the confidence born of many battles fought and won. They rode with absolute trust in their companions. Jack, Jason, and Poco Pete had been together for a long time, and each knew and recognized the courage and skill of the others in battling against long odds. Each one of them knew that if he fell, the others would never abandon him but would stand fast and fight to their last bullet and beyond. It had been said that Jack's men would gladly lay down their lives for him, but that was simply because his men knew that Jack would do the same for any one of them. The same trust and confidence bound the four Bailey brothers together. If you hurt one of them, then you hurt them all. It wasn't just family ties that bound them together, but also growing up in a hard land where the only thing they could count on was their trust in each other. This was the difference between them and the hired guns of Dan White. They fought to protect their family, friends, and livelihood, whereas the hired guns just fought for money. In the end, that was the difference between winning and losing.

They did not ride to the Porter ranch but rode straight for the town of Cedar Creek, and they rode painted for war. Halfway to the town, they saw a cloud of approaching dust, and they immediately split up and moved to opposite sides of the trail, waiting with their guns held ready. The approaching riders saw them from a distance and slowed their horses to a walk. As they came closer, the dust cloud dispersed, and Jack's group could see that there were ten men riding lathered horses, with their rifles held ready in their hands. Suddenly Poco Pete moved to the center of the trail and let loose a wild rebel yell, "Yeehaw!" The approaching riders immediately lowered their rifles, and one of them gave an answering yell. The riders drew up as they reached Jack's group, and the man in the lead gave Jack a salute and said, "Heard you were fighting another war, Major, and we figured to join up with you again."

"Good to see you again, Pike," said Jack with a smile. "There isn't time to bring you up to speed on events, but we are riding to town to end this war. There should be a dozen or more hired guns in town, and we are going to read them from the book." Pike said, "That would be about right, Major; we counted around fifteen men. They were in a group before the First Chance Saloon, and a torn and dusty man who looked like he had been in a war was giving them orders." Jason asked him, "You hear anything that was said?"

"Well, we kind-a eased around the crowd," replied Pike Roland. "But we did hear him tell the men to barricade the saloon and the jail." Mike said, "The jail is almost opposite the saloon, so he must mean to ambush us as we ride in." Roland laughed, "Friend, he obviously don't know the Major here. Even if I hadn't heard them orders, their ambush would have amounted to nothing." He looked back at his men, and they all laughed, and one of them said, "The Major here has a nose for an ambush. Why, I declare he can smell an ambush even before it's in place!" Jack held up his hand and said, "We'll catch up on old times later. Right now we got us a war to win. Let's ride!"

The cavalcade, now seventeen strong with the addition of the ten battle-hardened veterans, rode hard until they were on the outskirts of the town. Jack lifted his hand, and the riders drew up and waited. "Pete," Jack said. "You take Mike, Brian, and seven of our unit and go around the jail. The rest of us will move around the back of the saloon. You put three men in that land office next to the jail. It has a back entrance that you can use, and it has windows facing the jail. From there and from the rear, you'll have the jail sewed up tight." He turned to Jason and said, "Put Roland and the two remaining men at each of the three side windows of the saloon. Take Mark and Luke and enter through the back door." He turned to Poco Pete and told him, "When you're in place and ready, just whistle. You make your opening move only when you hear Jason's answering whistle and not before." Poco Pete nodded and then, shaking his head, stated, "You're going through the front door!" Jack simply said, "After you all hear Jason's whistle, count to ten slowly before opening the ball." They split up, and each group moved to take their positions.

Jack left Jason and the two Bailey brothers at the back door of the saloon and then pointed out the windows to Pike Roland and his two men. He then moved silently until he was at the corner of the front of the saloon. He scanned the front of the jail and the rest of the buildings on Main Street and noted the ends of two rifle barrels peeping through the window of the jail. He waited until he saw the three men running for the back of the land office building, and then, with his hat pulled down low, he turned and mounted the boardwalk. He began walking casually towards the front door of the saloon. In doing so, he wasn't being foolhardy, because he figured that the men in the jail would be looking for a cavalcade of riders and not a lone man walking to the saloon. They would assume that he was a resident of the town hunting a drink. Holding his rifle in his left hand, he paused briefly at the batwings to scan the room and counted ten men, with Dan White sitting at a table in the center. He heard Poco Pete's whistle and noted that there were no locals in the saloon, and even the barkeep was missing, with one of the hired guns behind the bar pouring drinks. Hearing Jason's answering whistle, he pushed the batwing doors open and walked in, immediately moving to the side away from the door. It took a moment for the men gathered there to realize that he was in the room, so silently did he move. Then they all turned and stared at him with puzzled expressions. Jack said mildly, "I'm from the Double M, and you are surrounded. My advice would be to drop your guns and ride out. But that's just me. You do whatever you've a mind to." Some of the men swore, and then they all went for their guns. Jack's rifle spoke once, and then his six-gun was blazing and men were dropping. From the back door, Jason and the others charged in, firing as they came, and from the side windows, three rifles spoke rapidly; and then there was silence. It was over almost before it began, and there were only three men still standing, although they were wounded and leaning against the bar for support. From the jail opposite, there was the sound of a small explosion and then silence.

As soon as Poco Pete heard Jason's whistle, he called out, "You men in the jailhouse! You're not setting an ambush; you've been ambushed. Come out without your guns, and you can ride out of town. Stay where you are, and I'm gonna throw in a stick of dynamite." It was Brian who had told Poco Pete that he still had some dynamite in his saddlebags. Quickly, Poco Pete had separated the sticks and attached a short fuse to a single stick. He figured that the entire bundle would bring down the jail building, whereas a single stick would just damage the occupants. A volley of shots was the response to his call, and Poco Pete shrugged and lit the fuse. He waited a moment and then threw the stick of dynamite through the back window of the jail. It exploded inside, and there were yells from the men, "Hold on! We're coming out unarmed! You people are just plumb crazy! Dynamite?"

CHAPTER 18
DAN WHITE

IN THE SALOON, JACK WAS SURPRISED TO SEE DAN White still sitting at the table. He hadn't been shot, but there was shock and disbelief writ large on his face as he stared at Jack. Dan White just could not believe that his plan was in shreds and that this one man was the cause of it. At first, his plan had seemed so easy and simple. Bring in enough hired guns and take over the entire area before reconstruction reached Texas. Then, as a big man in the locality, and as a supporter of the Union, he would land all the plum contracts and make a lot of money. But his plan went even further; in fact, it went up to the Governor's House. He intended to amass enough wealth and power to one day become the Governor of Texas, and Cedar Creek was to be his starting point. When he rode into town with his twenty hired guns and money to throw around, everything went his way at first. He had murdered and secretly buried old man Porter after forcing him to sign a bill of sale for his ranch holdings.

He soon realized that the Double M and the Rafter K weren't going to be easy marks, but he still wasn't worried. He figured it was just a matter of time before he forced them to fight in an open battle where his superior forces would finish them to the last man. His orders to his men were simple, "If you run into anyone belonging to the two ranches, then kill them. Force them into a gun battle if you must, but kill them." Matt Duncan, Nat Hardy, and Leon Mendoza were the spearheads of the plan as they were reputed to be the fastest guns in the West. Black Wind was the ace up his sleeve, and he intended to use him later on to hunt down and kill from ambush the owners of the ranches and their families, as he knew that that was something Matt Duncan and Leon Mendoza would not agree to.

With the killing of Billy and Clyde Hadden in town, everything seemed to be progressing as per his plan. And then that stranger rode into town! He had disabled two of his men and had saved the life of Bruce McCullough. When he was informed that Bruce was in town, he saw an opportunity to force Ryan out into the open. His orders were to stage a fight between Bruce and one of the drifters who hung around town, and then his men would gun down Bruce. It had all been arranged, and from what he had heard, it was going smoothly until the stranger took a hand in the game.

He knew his name now, Jack Donovan. He also knew something about him, but nothing much really, because Matt Duncan and Nat Hardy had told him, "The man's like a ghost! There are rumors enough about him, but no hard facts; and he doesn't exactly advertise himself. But we'll take care of him. You just rest easy on that one." But that was days ago, and his days of easy resting disappeared as Jack Donovan came to town and gunned down Leon Mendoza and killed Jake Rawlings in a knife fight. He had then taken away Nat Hardy's gun and had slapped him silly in front of all the men Dan White had sent to arrest him. Dan White had had enough, and he had given Black Wind his orders: hunt down and kill Jack Donovan. Black Wind had set out early in the morning before dawn to do just that, but by the afternoon, he was in town getting his wrist sewn up by the town's sawbones before drifting out of town. The Doc said that Black Wind would never use that hand again with full strength.

Now he stared at Jack and said, "Who the hell are you and where did you spring from? Give me half a chance and I'll make you pay for spoiling my perfect plan!" Jack shrugged and told him, "Draw whenever you're ready." Slowly Dan White stood up and said, "I'm not a gunslinger and I'm going to unbuckle my gun belt now." Very carefully he unbuckled his gun belt and let it drop. Then he flexed his fists and said, "If you have the guts, we can settle this man to man. Or maybe you like hiding behind your guns!" Jack shook his head in disgust and grimaced. He drew his six-shooter and, pointing it at Dan White, said, "I'm hiding behind my guns? This is coming from a man who has been hiding behind so many hired guns all this while! Now that you've lost out, you think you can just throw a challenge, and I'll get into a fistfight with you. Obviously, you rate yourself highly in fist fighting, or you wouldn't throw a challenge." He sighed and then said, "You must think everyone else is a moron. Tell me, why should I bother to accept your challenge? I will give you a challenge instead. You put your gun on the table and keep your hand on it. My gun will be in my holster. Whenever you're ready, all you have to do is pick up your gun and shoot. Do you have the guts, or are you just a yellow-bellied blowhard who hires others to do his killing?" Jack holstered his gun and told Jason, "See that no one interferes." He told Dan White, "If you can beat me, you can ride out of here a free man, and no one will stop you."

Dan White licked his lips and looked down at his gun and then looked at Jack standing casually, waiting for him to move. It seemed to Dan White to be a stupid challenge that Jack could not possibly win, yet some of the rumors about this man that Matt Duncan had narrated made him hesitate. Was this man really that fast? "I'm no gunslinger," he repeated. "But I'll fight you with my bare hands, and you can make the rules!" Jack asked Jason, "Why is it that bullies always think that others will fall for their challenge? They will only throw a challenge when they think the odds are on their side to win. Yet they assume that it will be accepted." He turned to Dan White and said, "Be that as it may, I'll fight you because you are the one responsible for killing Billy and Clyde Hadden, even though you didn't pull the trigger. Walk out the front door, and we'll do her in the street." A light gleamed in Dan White's eyes. He had never been beaten in a knockdown, drag-out, knuckle-and-skull, no-holds-barred fight. On the waterfront and on ships, he had learnt every dirty trick in the book and had patented some of his own. He always won because when his opponent made a move, he knew all about it and knew all the counters to it as well. No one had ever taken him by a surprise move, and he was confident that no one ever would. He would take pleasure in tearing this man apart with his bare hands. He removed his shirt and flexed his muscles, and everyone could see that he was built like a bull with a hard, well-muscled body, and his hands were calloused with scarred knuckles. He walked out the front door and stood in the center of the street, still flexing and bending his body to stretch and loosen his muscles. Then he shoved his hands in his pockets and stood waiting for Jack, who had followed him out along with Jason and the Bailey brothers. From the other side of the street, Poco Pete, Mike, Brian and the rest appeared with guns drawn. Their prisoners had started to make their way to their horses when they realized that a fistfight was in the offing and pleaded with Poco Pete, "This we got to watch! We've heard of Dan White's reputation in a fistfight, and a brutal reputation it is. I swear we'll ride as soon as she's over!" Poco Pete shrugged and remarked, "Okay, this won't take long anyway." The man looked at him and said, "You're saying your friend can't fight? Mister, was I you, I'd call this off right now. Dan White will murder him for sure!" Poco Pete just shrugged, and the prisoners looked at him

THE LEGEND OF JACK DONOVAN

in disbelief. Was this man going to let his friend be beaten to death?

Jack had removed his gun belt and handed it over with his rifle to Luke. "Take care of this," he said. "I'll be right back." He walked out to the center of the street and stood facing Dan White, who had a malicious grin on his face.

"I'm going to kill you!" Dan said. "I'm going to wipe the street with you! This is gonna be the sweetest payback ever!"

Jack said with disgust, "You're gonna kill me with your mouth?"

Snarling, Dan took his hands out of his pockets and charged him. Everyone could see that he had wicked-looking spiked knuckle dusters on. He took a mighty swing at Jack's head, but his hand met only empty air. Jack's head had moved back in a flash, and as the force of the blow carried Dan past him, Jack's hand lashed out sideways. He didn't hit with a fist but with the edge of his palm, and Dan White fell sprawling in the dust on his face. His neck felt as if it had been hit with a rifle butt, but he immediately rolled over twice, expecting Jack to put the boot to him when he was down. Completing his roll, he jumped up to find that Jack had not moved. He just couldn't believe it! If Jack had fallen, he would have finished him with his boots because that was the way he fought. He couldn't believe that this man hadn't taken advantage of him falling down. But the blow to the neck had made him wary, as he realized that Jack could hit, and hit hard.

He slowly began circling and coming closer to Jack, but Jack just kept shifting his stance to keep facing him, doing nothing else. He didn't even have his hands up in the usual boxing stance but just stood there, breathing evenly and watching Dan White.

When he was close enough, Dan White suddenly charged in a bull rush with the intention of knocking Jack down with his superior weight; but again, he found himself face down in the street, eating dust. To the onlookers, it seemed that one moment Jack was standing right in front of Dan's charge, and the next, he had just shifted out of the way, and as Dan went past him, he stuck his leg out and tripped him. But Dan White had been knocked down before, and he always got up, and he always won. Now he pulled himself up and snarled, "Okay, now you're going to get it, and no amount of fancy footwork is gonna save you!" He walked slowly up to Jack with his hands ready to swing, but when he was still out of arm's reach, Jack's foot suddenly lashed out and upwards and hit Dan full in the face. Once more, Dan was flat on the ground, although this time on his back. The speed of Jack's movement and the height that his leg had reached had the spectators gasping in awe. This was something they had never seen before, and they were silent as they watched.

There wasn't the usual shouting and heckling from the sidelines, which was common in any fistfight. This time, there was only an awed silence. Dan White pulled himself up once more and was shocked to see Jack still just standing and waiting for him to get up. He tried to speak and winced as he realized that his jaw was broken. But for all his faults, Dan White was a tough man, and he wasn't about to give up. He advanced warily, and this time, he got within arm's reach as Jack just stood there and did not move. He threw a vicious hook, which started from his knees and would have flattened any man had it landed, especially with the murderous knuckle duster. But in a flash of movement, Jack caught his wrist and twisted sideways and down and then up, which turned Dan almost fully around, and then Jack turned with Dan's extended arm on his shoulder and threw him over his head. Dan was again face down in the street. He shook himself and jumped up snarling, and rushed Jack again, but this time Jack did not move away. In a blur of movement, he hit Dan in the solar plexus with a closed fist that had the knuckle of the middle finger extended. The breath left Dan

White in a rush, and then he was hit with the same extended knuckle on his upper lip, just below his nose, and the upward force of the blow threw his head back and broke his nose. With his head thrown back, his neck was exposed, and Jack hit him savagely on his throat with the edge of his palm, and Dan White dropped like a felled steer and lay still, with blood pouring out of his open mouth.

Jack then calmly walked over and collected his gun belt from Luke and swung it around his hips.

The silence was deafening as the men watching just could not believe that they actually saw what they had seen. One of them asked in almost a whisper, "What the hell happened? Is he dead?"

It was Jason who answered, "He's dead all right, and this war is over. If any of you are still here when I finish counting to ten, I'll gut shoot you!"

Nobody doubted him, and the remaining men ran for their horses, and soon there was only a dust cloud and the pounding of hooves as they left town in a rush.

The Bailey brothers and Jack's army unit all gathered around him, and Jason said, "That's only the second time I've seen you do that move after that run-in with that renegade in the war."

Jack said softly, "That was for Billy and Clyde. Now they can rest in peace!"

EPILOGUE

Word of the Cedar Creek war spread far and wide and the legend of Lightning Hands was told over many a campfire and lost nothing in the telling. When curiosity to see the man known as Lightning Hands brought men to Cedar Creek, they were told that he had left town soon after the fighting ended and no one knew his whereabouts. The people of Cedar Creek kept their secret, and Jack Donovan finally stopped drifting and settled down to ranching. He married Beth, and in time they had two sons, the first of whom they named Ned and the second they named Billy. Pike Roland and the rest of Jack's old unit were offered jobs on the Double M and the Rafter K. Roland and five men accepted, while the rest went back to their hometowns and families. Pike Roland became the town Marshal of Cedar Creek. Jason Montana and Poco Pete stayed on, and Jason became the foreman of the Double M. Jason eventually married, and a home was built on the ranch for his family. Poco Pete never married. Bruce married Betsy Bailey, and the two ranches became more united than ever. As for the Bailey brothers...well, that's another story!

ABOUT THE AUTHOR

Terence Newnes was born in south India. He dropped out of college and during the 70s and 80s he worked in fabrication, machine shops, and tool rooms. He then worked a short stint in Ethiopia. At the age of 43 he became a certified medical transcriptionist and worked in Toledo, Ohio as a medical transcriptionist, editor, and finally shift team lead. He started his own business of call center and data entry in 2006. During the pandemic and lockdown he lost his business and went broke, but he never lost hope. He started writing, which was a childhood dream, and he has never stopped.

To learn more about Terence Newnes and discover more Next Chapter authors, visit our website at www.nextchapter.pub.

The Legend of Jack Donovan
ISBN: 978-4-82419-844-0

Published by
Next Chapter
2-5-6 SANNO
SANNO BRIDGE
143-0023 Ota-Ku, Tokyo
+818035793528

28th September 2024

www.ingramcontent.com/pod-product-compliance
Lightning Source LLC
LaVergne TN
LVHW040102080526
838202LV00045B/3742